M.Y.T.H. İNC. LINK

M.Y.T.H.
INC. LINK

Robert Asprin

A LEGEND BOOK

Published by Arrow Books Limited
20 Vauxhall Bridge Road, London SW1V 2SA

An imprint of the Random Century Group

London Melbourne Sydney Auckland
Johannesburg and agencies throughout
the world

First published by Donning Company/Publishers, 1986

Legend edition 1991

Printed and bound in Great Britain by
Cox & Wyman Ltd, Reading, Berkshire

ISBN 0 09 980420 4

Author's Introduction

The series of books loosely referred to throughout the known dimensions as **The Myth Adventures of Aahz and Skeeve** has been growing steadily in popularity since they premiered back in 1978. (Actually, you probably don't have to be told this, as you are already holding a volume in your hands. The ones who need to be informed are those who would never *dream* of picking up a fantasy book . . . like that guy in the next aisle browsing through mysteries, or your roommate. So what you want to do is tap them on the shoulder or over the head, and . . .)

Excuse me! I tend to get excited and digress when there's the smell of money in the air . . . especially if it's moving away. Where was I?

Books . . . growing in popularity . . . oh, yes!

The question I am asked most often as a writer is not "Where do you get your ideas?", but rather, "Is there going to be another Myth book?" The answer, for a while anyway, is a definite "Yes!" After completing **Little Myth Marker** (#6 in the series . . .collect 'em all!) I signed a contract with Donning/Starblaze for an additional six books, of which this is the first. While we're still "discussing" if they will be written at the rate of one or two a year, it *is* sure at this point that the series will be around for a while.

I realized after completing the manuscript for this volume that the title might be unclear to the casual reader.

This is a terrible thing to realize so close to publication, particularly since the book has already been promoted under that title, so it's too late to change it. In desperation, I'm resorting to the cheap device of an author's intro to attempt to clarify things.

#7 is titled **M.Y.T.H. Inc. Link** because it marks a definite change in the series from the first six and therefore "links" the beginning of the series to what comes after. (Cute, eh? Confusing, but cute.) Unfortunately, most of the changes involve the writer, and, as such, may not be readily apparent to the reader. In a vain attempt to alleviate that situation, I thought I would take advantage of this breaking point in the series to give the reader a little insight into the mind of a writer and how a series, specifically this one, comes to exist. If you couldn't care less, feel free to skip directly into the main body of the book (as the rest of this introduction contains nothing you need to read) and (hopefully) enjoy it.

Writers not only "live" what they write, they occasionally use that fact to regulate their actual lives. That is, if they are feeling "down," sometimes writing something "up" can improve their mood. This was how the first Myth book came into existence.

At the time (1976) I was writing my first novel, **Cold Cash War**, for St. Martin's Press. That particular book is a grim little number about corporate wars, and contains occasional scenes that can only be described as grisly. Wounded mercenaries burying themselves while still alive to rob the other side of the body count and executives arranging to have their rivals shot down in the streets were the norm in that universe. It was an interesting project, and, as it was my first, I could really get wrapped up in it. Unfortunately, I was still working full time at a nine-to-five job and had a wife and two kids. It was unfortunate in that I discovered that if I wrote **Cold Cash** for too many nights at a stretch, I'd start looking at my fellow office workers, not to mention passersby on the sidewalk and my own family, as targets or attackers. This is not the best condition to ensure one's continued mental health.

I decided I needed another writing project to use as a break for **Cold Cash** (if you just stop writing, you never get back to it!), preferably something a bit lighter. To that end, I started building the idea for my next book.

Being a fan of Conan and Kane and that crowd, I had always wanted to try my hand at Heroic Fantasy, and this seemed like as good a time as any. The field had been getting increasingly solemn and grandiose, and to my eye was long overdue for a good lampooning. (Anything or anyone who falls into the trap of taking themselves too seriously is fair game for this, and, fortunately for writers such as myself, there is no shortage of targets these days.)

First, I needed a main character. Since Heroic Fantasy was already loaded with brawny barbarian swordsmen hunting wizards, I decided to go to the opposite extreme and do my story from the point of view of a magician. To keep it interesting, he had to be fairly incompetent . . . say, maybe an apprentice. It's always helpful to give your lead character an associate or sidekick. This allows you to use dialogue to impart information to the reader without resorting to lengthy introspection. For a confidant to a magician . . . why not a demon? To contrast personalities, I'd have to make him as snorky and unpleasant as my lead is nice.

Right about here, fate took a hand. I have always been a fan of the Bob Hope/Bing Crosby "Road" movies, and it turned out that at the same time I was tinkering

with these new characters, there was a weeklong festival
of the entire set of those films on television. Of course,
as a dedicated writer working on a book with a deadline,
I was immune to such temptation, right? If you believe
that, you have a lot to learn about writers . . . or at least
this writer. Each evening found me camped in front of
the idiot tube to catch one more round of the particular
brand of insanity those movies abound in. To combat
the guilts of feeling *totally* irresponsible, I kept a notepad
on my lap so I could "work on character development"
during the commercials. Trying to switch moods back
and forth between the "Road" movies and **Cold Cash**
was impossible, so it made more sense to be futzing
around with *my* comedy while watching theirs. In the
process, the bantering swindlers whose plans always land
them in inordinate amounts of trouble wandered off the
screen and onto my notepad . . . and the characters of
Aahz and Skeeve started to take shape.

By the time **Cold Cash** was done, I was ready to
present Aahz and Skeeve as a proposal for my next book.
When I mentioned this to my agent, however, I discovered there was a minor detail I had overlooked.
"Humor doesn't sell!" I was told. "We're trying to get
your career launched right now, and you need a really
strong book to follow **Cold Cash**! Got anything else?"
This attitude startled me, but it was easily confirmed. A
brief glance at a year's worth of *Publishers Weekly*
showed that indeed, unless you were Erma Bombeck
with a national following via a syndicated column, humor
simply did not show on the best-seller lists. Consequently, I went with another project, **The Bug Wars**,
and relegated the Aahz and Skeeve proposal to a bottom
drawer.

There it remained while I spent roughly a year working

on **The Bug Wars**. Then one evening in late 1977 my phone rang. It was Kelly Freas, the artist who had done the cover painting for the issue of *Analog* in which an excerpt of **Cold Cash** had been published, and a longtime friend from the convention circuit. He explained that he was starting a new line of books (Starblaze) with a Virginia-based publishing house (Donning) and was currently soliciting submissions. Did I have any unpublished manuscripts lying around? Needless to say, I was flattered, but I had to admit the only thing I had ready for submission was a humor presentation . . . and he wouldn't want that, would he? There was a noticeable hesitation; then he suggested I send it in so he could take a look at it.

In an impressively short time, he got back to me with his reaction: He liked the characters and the setting, but felt the story was weak. If I thought I could come up with another story line, he'd cut me a contract. Being as greedy and prone to flattery as the next person, I agreed. When I discovered he needed it "just as soon as possible so that it can be one of our premiere titles," I was a bit less confident, but said I would give it my best shot. What the heck, I was on a roll.

To give you an idea of how much I had gotten caught up in the momentum of the deal, it wasn't until then that I realized none of this had been cleared with my agent. With a certain degree of abashed trepidation, I phoned my agent and explained the situation. There was a weighty pause, then he agreed. "I can see where you'd want to do a favor for an old buddy," he said, "and you might as well give him something that isn't going to go anywhere." I always thrive on encouragement.

So, I had characters, a setting, a contract, but no story. Facing an ASAP deadline and pressured by my agent to "finish it off quick and get back to serious writing," I resorted to a time-honored resource for writers under pressure . . . I stole a story line! Actually, I rationalized it rather neatly. This book is a parody, right? Why not take a ''done to death'' story line and do it one more time with the tongue-in-cheek respect it deserves? (This was the start of a pattern, but more about that later . . . .)

With a sort of preordained story line and characters I already knew like they were family, the writing went fairly quickly. To be precise, I wrote the thing front to back in five weeks while working full-time days. As an added bonus, I tossed in chapter quotes. After all, the books I was parodying usually had chapter quotes for songs or characters invented by the author for just that purpose, so why not do the same for mine? (When the book became a series, I found out ''why not!'' If you do it in the first volume, the readers expect it in subsequent volumes. It's a lot harder to come up with 120 cute quotes than it is to invent 20! I often spend more time of the *##!! quotes than I do writing the book!)

The manuscript went in and was accepted without a hitch. (There are certain advantages to dealing with artists who are editors. They tend to leave your writing alone!) The problem which arose was, of all things, on the title. I had always had problems titling books, and this one had been no exception. What I had finally come up with was **The Demon And I**. Doesn't make it, Kelly said. I promised to try to think of an alternative. Three weeks later, press time for the catalog was upon us, and I was still trying to think of a better title. On the day of the noon deadline, I was sitting on the phone with Kelly at 11:45, still trying to come up with a title. **Demon on Square One**? How about **Demon at Large**? Better, but not funny.

Funny . . . funny . . . My mind started darting over

lines and movie titles from classic comedy. What do you think of **Another Fine Mess**? Hmmm . . . Kelly put down the phone and bounced the title off his wife, Polly, whose taste exceeds the sum of ours combined. He was back in a moment. Did I say **Another Fine Mess**, or **Another Fine *Myth***? I confirmed the former. Another conference. Well, it wasn't red-hot, but it seemed to be the best we had to come up with. They'd go with that.

Three hours later (and that much closer to sundown, when I normally start thinking,) my brain started to turn over like a car engine on a cold morning. **Another Fine Myth** . . . **Hit or Myth** . . . **Myth Conceptions!** I hurriedly grabbed the phone and called Kelly back.

On the off chance he wanted to buy another book with these characters, I explained, and definitely if there was a possibility of turning it into a series, the "Myth" bit could come in handy to tie the titles together! In fact, it was a natural to use **Myth Conceptions** as a title for the first book, and hold **Another Fine Myth** for the sequel! How solid was that noon deadline?

It turned out the noon deadline had been real. (A sure sign of an inexperienced editor. The real pros *never* tell you the truth about when they need a manuscript or title, just to allow time for the wayward creative minds to miss the supposed deadline and still hit the real deadline!) He did, however, like the idea. While we couldn't change the title from **Another Fine Mess** to **Myth Conceptions**, we could change it to **Another Fine Myth** and claim a typo in the catalog! We'd just hold the **Myth Conceptions** title for the second one . . . we *were* talking about doing a second one, weren't we? Whoops!

So the series was launched. Over the years, Donning kept contracting them from me, usually one at a time, and I kept swiping plots to parody. The mad magician out to take over the world, the select force against an army, the master heist, the big game, the war against organized crime . . . all the old familiar chestnuts (which I follow avidly myself) were dragged out and run over one more time. Some strange things happened along the way, however.

I had promised myself from the beginning that Skeeve would grow and develop as the series continued. This would theoretically keep me from falling into the trap of telling the same story and using the same gags over and over again. Rereading the manuscripts as they piled up, however, I began to realize how much of my own growth and development was easing onto the pages. Since I started writing the Myth series, I have been raising (or, more accurately, assisting in raising between books) two children of my own, and experiencing all the trials and doubts that go with parenthood. I went from being a full-time cost accountant with a regular paycheck to a full-time writer with a spastic cash flow, and hence became even more concerned with money than I had been when it was plentiful. I tried to start a corporation of my own, only to have it fold within the first six months. With the success of the books, I even experienced the heady sensation of being a minor celebrity and having total strangers recognize my name. All these experiences and more became a part of Skeeve's development and the evolution of his relationship with his rat-pack of friends. Because of this, the friends themselves began to take on new life and dimensions until they began crowding in on the central story of Skeeve.

This brings us to **M.Y.T.H. Inc. Link.** (Remember? I started out tell you about that? It's the book you're holding right now.) In this volume the readers get a chance to see the Myth universe and, more importantly,

Skeeve through eyes other than those belonging to the central character. Lest the diehard Skeeve fans panic, let me hasten to assure them I haven't finished with Skeeve's viewpoint . . . not by a long shot! In the upcoming volumes, however, the Skeeve-narrated volumes will have the regular "Myth" titles, and those from other viewpoints will be designated by the "M.Y.T.H. Inc." label. This particular volume has sections of both, hence the "Link" between old and new formats. Get it? Oh well, maybe it will become clearer after you read this one.

The other major change which is occurring is that with the contractual assurance that there will be future volumes, I can work a larger canvas as a storyteller (yes, that is a mixed metaphor) than I was able to when planning one book at a time. Not every story element has to be resolved within a single book, and setups for future stories and situations can be seeded in. Among other things, this means that I will probably be moving away from the predictable "old plot parodies" I have been indulging in in the past, and creating situations and tales unique to the Myth universe and its inhabitants.

(If that sounds like you'll have to buy every volume to stay abreast of what's happening, it's not entirely accidental. I've learned a lot from co-editing **Thieves' World**™, too!)

The new path I have chosen for *Myth* and myself is extremely challenging to an author, but one I feel is a necessary option to either shutting the series down or "cranking out one more of the same." There are those in both the book and comic industries who insist that series readers rapidly become addicted to the status quo, and will protest or rebel against any attempt to change it. I can only hope the loyal *Myth* readers find the new directions as enjoyable and intriguing as I do. If not, tough! This is the way it's going to be for at least five more books.

While I can occasionally sound very uncaring and set in my ways, like any author I am always curious about reader reactions . . . particularly when instituting a major pattern change. In case you weren't aware of it, you can always write me (or any author, assuming they're alive) in care of the publisher. If you'd like a larger forum in which to air your feelings, there's always the Myth-Adventures Fan Club, P.O. Box 95, Sutter, CA 95982 (blatant plug!) with their quarterly publication. Please include a stamped, self-addressed envelope.

In closing, I would like to sincerely thank all the *Myth* readers for their loyalty and interest over the years. All your letters are read (even if I don't get a chance to answer them all) and deeply appreciated. After all the earlier warnings from my (ex-) agent and the lack of interest from other publishers, the appearance of the *Myth* books on genre and chain-store best-seller lists has not only increased my stature in the field to where I am now offered the six-book contracts that allow me to experiment with new concepts, but combined with the popularity of Piers Anthony's **Xanth** books has forced publishers to review their attitudes toward humorous fantasy. The door has been opened for a new wave of talented writers, whose efforts are even now available on the stands. For these hitherto unrecognized humorists as well as for myself and the *Myth* gang, again, I thank you.

—Robert Lynn Asprin
Ann Arbor, 1986

Chapter One:

"Petty crime is the scourge of business today."
—D. LOREAN

I ACTUALLY LIKED our new office facilities better than
the old. Even though Aahz had argued hard to keep the
Even Odds as a bar (read "money-making venture"),
the rest of us ganged up on him and insisted that since
we had an extra building it would make more sense to
remodel it into offices than to keep trying to do business
out of our home. I mean, who really needs a lot of
strangers traipsing in and out of your private life all the
time? That practice had already landed us in trouble once,
and the memory of that escapade was what finally convinced my old mentor to go along with the plan.

Of course, remodeling was more of a hassle than I
had expected, even after getting one of the local religious
temples to do the carpentry. Even working cheap they
were more expensive than I had imagined, and the hours
they kept . . . but I digress.

I had a large office now, with a desk, "in" basket,
Day-Timers Scheduler, visitor chairs, the whole nine

1

yards. As I said, I liked it a lot. What I didn't like was
the title that went with it . . . to wit, President.

That's right. Everybody insisted that since incorporat-
ing our merry band of misfits was my idea, I was the
logical choice for titular head of the organization. Even
Aahz betrayed me, proclaiming it was a great idea, though
to my eye he was hiding a snicker when he said it. If I
had known my suggestion would lead to this, believe me
I would have kept my mouth shut.

Don't get me wrong, the crew is great! If I were going
to lead a group, I couldn't ask for a nicer, more loyal
bunch than the one currently at my disposal. Of course,
there might be those who would argue the point with
me. A trollop, a troll, two gangsters, a moll, and a Pervert
. . . excuse me, Pervect . . . an overweight vamp, and
a baby dragon might not seem like the ideal team to the
average person. They didn't to me when I first met them.
Still, they've been unswerving in their support of me
over the years, and together we've piled up an impressive
track record. No, I'd rather stick with the rat-pack I
know, however strange, than trust my fate to anyone
else, no matter how qualified they might seem. If anything, from time to time I wonder what they think of me
and wish I could peek inside their heads to learn their
opinions. Whatever they think, they stick around . . .
and that's what counts.

It isn't the crew that makes me edgy . . . it's the title.
You see, as long as I can remember, I've always thought
that being a leader was the equivalent of walking around
with a large bulls-eye painted on your back. Basically
the job involves holding the bag for a lot of people instead
of just for yourself. If anything goes wrong, you end up
being to blame. Even if someone else perpetrated the
foul-up, as the leader you're responsible. On the off

chance things go right, all you really feel is guilty for taking the credit for someone else's work. All in all, it seems to me to be a no-win, thankless position, one that I would much rather delegate to someone else while I had fun in the field. Unfortunately, everyone else seemed to have the same basic opinion, and as the least experienced member of the crew I was less adept at coming up with reasons to dodge the slot than the others. Consequently, I became the President of M.Y.T.H. Inc. (That's Magical Young Trouble-shooting Heroes. Don't blame me. I didn't come up with the name), an association of magicians and trouble-shooters dedicated to simultaneously helping others and making money.

Our base of operations was the Bazaar at Deva, a well-known rendezvous for magic dealing that was the crossroads of the dimensions. As might be imagined, in an environment like that, there was never a shortage of work.

I had barely gotten settled for the morning when there was a light rap on the door of my office and Bunny stuck her head in.

"Busy, Boss?"

"Well . . ."

She was gone before I could finish formulating a vague answer. This wasn't unusual. Bunny acted as my secretary and always knew more about what I had on the docket than I did. Her inquiries as to my schedule were usually made out of politeness or to check to be sure I wasn't doing something undignified before ushering a client into the office.

"The Great Skeeve will see you now," she said, gesturing grandly to her charge. "In the future, I'd suggest you make an appointment so you won't be kept waiting."

The Deveel Bunny was introducing seemed a bit slimy, even for a Deveel. His bright red complexion was covered with unhealthy-looking pink blotches, and his face was contorted into a permanent leer, which he directed at Bunny's back as she left the room.

Now, there's no denying that Bunny's one of the more attractive females I've ever met, but there was something unwholesome about the attention this dude was giving her. With an effort, I tried to quell the growing dislike I was feeling toward the Deveel. A client was a client, and we were in business to help people in trouble, not make moral judgments on them.

"Can I help you?" I said, keeping my voice polite.

That brought the Deveel's attention back to me, and he extended a hand across the desk.

"So you're the Great Skeeve, eh? Pleased to meet you. Been hearing some good things about your work. Say, you really got a great setup. I especially like that little number you got working as a receptionist. Might even try to hire her away from you. The girl's obviously loaded with talent."

Looking at his leer and wink, I somehow couldn't bring myself to shake his hand.

"Bunny is my administrative assistant," I said carefully. "She is also a stockholder in the company. She earns her position with her skills, not with her looks."

"I bet she does," the Deveel winked again. "I'd love to get a sample of those skills someday."

That did it.

"How about right now?" I smiled, then raised my voice slightly. "Bunny? Could you come in here for a moment?"

She appeared almost at once, ignoring the Deveel's

leer as she moved to my desk.

"Yes, sir?"

"Bunny, you forgot to brief me on this client. Who is he?"

She arched one eyebrow and shot a sideways glance at the Deveel. We rarely did our briefings in front of clients. Our eyes met again and I gave her a small nod to confirm my request.

"His name is Bane," she said with a shrug. "He's known to run a small shop here at the Bazaar selling small novelty magic items. His annual take from that operation is in the low six figures."

"Hey! That's pretty good," the Deveel grinned.

Bunny continued as if she hadn't heard.

"He also has secret ownership of three other businesses, and partial ownership of a dozen more. Most notable is a magic factory which supplies shops in this and other dimensions. It's located in a sub-dimension accessible through the office of his shop, and employs several hundred workers. The estimated take from that factory alone is in the mid seven figure range annually."

The Deveel had stopped leering.

"How did you know all that?" he demanded. "That's supposed to be secret!"

"He also fancies himself to be a lady-killer, but there is little evidence to support his claim. The female companions he is seen in public with are paid for their company, and none have lasted more than a week. It seems they feel the money is insufficient for enduring his revolting personality. Foodwise, he has a weakness for broccoli."

I turned a neutral smile on the deflated Deveel.

" . . . And *that*, sir, is the talent that earns Bunny her

job. Did you enjoy your sample?''

"She's wrong about the broccoli,'' Bane said weakly.
"I hate broccoli.''

I raised an eyebrow at Bunny, who winked back at me.

"Noted,'' she said. "Will there be anything else,
Boss?''

"Stick around, Bunny. I'll probably need your help
quoting Mr. Bane a price for our services . . . that is, if
he ever gets around to telling us what his problem is.''

That brought the Deveel out of his shocked trance.

"I'll tell you what the problem is! Miss Bunny here
was dead right when she said my magic factory is my
prize holding. The trouble is that someone's robbing me
blind! I'm losing a fortune to pilferage!''

"What percentage loss?'' Bunny said, suddenly attentive.

"Pushing fourteen percent . . . up from six last year.''

"Are we talking retail or cost value?''

"Cost.''

"What's your actual volume loss?''

"Less than eight percent. They know exactly what
items to go after . . . small, but expensive.''

I sat back and tried to look wise. They had lost me
completely about two laps into the conversation, but
Bunny seemed to know what she was doing, so I gave
her her head.

"Everybody I've sent in to investigate gets tagged as
a company spy before they even sit down,'' Bane was
saying. "Now, the word I get is that your crew has some
contacts in organized crime, and I was figuring . . .''

He let his voice trail off, then shrugged as if he was
embarrassed to complete the thought.

Bunny looked over at me, and I could tell she was

trying to hide a smile. She was the niece of Don Bruce, the Mob's Fairy Godfather, and it always amused her to encounter the near-superstitious awe outsiders felt toward her uncle's organization.

"I think we can help you," I said carefully. "Of course, it will cost."

"How much?" Bane countered, settling back for what was acknowledged throughout the dimensions as a Deveel's specialty . . . haggling.

In response, Bunny scribbled something quickly on her notepad, then tore the sheet off and handed it to Bane.

The Deveel glanced at it and blanched a light pink.

"WHAT!! That's robbery and you know it!"

"Not when you consider what the losses are costing you," Bunny said sweetly. "Tell you what. If you'd rather, we'll take a few points in your factory . . . say, half the percentage reduction in pilferage once we take the case?"

Bane went from pink to a volcanic red in the space of a few heartbeats.

"All right! It's a deal . . . at the original offer!"

I nodded slightly.

"Fine. I'll assign a couple of agents to it immediately."

"Wait a minute! I'm paying prices like these and I'm not even getting the services of the head honcho? What are you trying to pull here? I want . . ."

"The Great Skeeve stands behind every M.Y.T.H. Inc. contract," Bunny interrupted. "If you wish to contract his personal services, the price would be substantially higher . . . like, say, controlling interest?"

"All right, all right! I get the message!" the Deveel said. "Send in your agents. They just better be good, that's all. At these rates, I expect results!''

With that, he slammed out of the office, leaving Bunny and me alone.

"How much *did* you charge him?"

"Just our usual fees."

"Really?"

"Well . . . I did add in a small premium 'cause I didn't like him. Any objections?"

"No. Just curious is all."

"Say, Boss. Would you mind including me in this assignment? It shouldn't take too long, and this one's got me a little curious."

"Okay . . . but not as lead operative. I want to be able to pull you back here if things get hairy in the office. Let your partner run the show."

"No problem. Who are you teaming me with?"

I leaned back in my chair and smiled.

"Can't you guess? The client wants organized crime, he *gets* organized crime!"

Guido's Tale

"Guido, are you *sure* you've got your instructions right?"

That is Bunny talkin'. For some reason the Boss has deemed it wise to delegate to me her company for this job. Now this is okay with me, as Bunny is more than enjoyable to look at and a swell head to boot, which is to say she is smarter than me, which is a thing I do not say about many people, guys or dolls.

The only trepidation with which I view this pairin' is that as swell as she is, Bunny also has a marked tendency to nag whenever a job is on. This is because she is handicapped with a problem, which is that she has her cap set for the Boss. Now we are all aware of this, for it was apparent as the nose on your face from the day they first encountered. Even the Boss could see this, which is sayin' sumpin', for while I admire the Boss as an organizer, he is a little thick between the ears when it comes to skirts. To show you what I mean, once he was aware that Bunny did indeed entertain notions on his bod, his response was to half faint from the nervousness. This is from a guy I've watched take on vampires and werewolf types, not to mention Don Bruce himself, without so much as battin' an eye. Like I say, dolls is not his strong suit.

Anyway, I was talkin' about Bunny and her problem. She finally managed to convince the Boss that she wasn't really tryin' to pair up with him, but was just interested in furtherin' her career as a business type. Now this was a blatant lie, and we all knew it . . . even though it seems to have fooled the Boss. Even that green bum, Aahz, could see what Bunny was up to. (This surprised me a bit, for I always thought his main talent was makin' loud noises.) All that Bunny was doin' was switchin' from one come-on to another. Her overall motivational goal has never changed.

The unfortunate circumstances of this is that instead of wooin' the Boss with her bod, which as I have said is outstandin', she is now tryin' to win his admiration with what a sharp cookie she is. This should not be overly difficult, as Bunny is one shrewd operator, but like all dolls she feels she has limited time in which to accomplish her objective before her looks run out, so she is tryin' extra hard to make sure the Boss notices her.

This unfortunately can make her a real headache in the posterior regions to work with. She is so afraid that someone else will mess up her performance record that

she can drive a skilled worker such as myself up a prover-
bial tree with her nervous double-check chatter. Still,
she is a swell doll and we are all pullin' for her, so we
put up with it.

"Yes, Bunny," I sez.

" 'Yes, Bunny' what?"

"Yes, Bunny, I'm sure I got my instructions right."

"Then repeat them back to me."

"Why?"

"Guido!"

When Bunny gets that tone in her voice, there is little
else to do but to humor her. This is in part because part
of my job is to be supportive to my teammate when on
an assignment, but also because Bunny has a mean left
hook when she feels you are givin' her grief. My cousin
Nunzio chanced to discover this fact one time before he
was informed that she was Don Bruce's niece, and as he
had a jaw like an anvil against which I have had occasion
to injure my fist with noticeable results, I have no desire
to confirm for myself the strength of the blow with which
she decked him. Consequently I decided to comply with
her rather annoying request.

"The Boss wants us to find out how the goods of a
particular establishment is successfully wanderin' off the
premises without detection," I sez. "To that end I am
to intermingle with the workers as one of them to see if
I can determine how this is bein' accomplished."

"And . . ." she sez, givin' me the hairy eyeball.

". . . And you are to do the same, only with the office
types. At the end of a week we are to regroup in order
that we may compare observations and see if we are
perhaps barkin' up the wrong tree."

"And . . ." she sez again, lookin' a trifle agitated.

At this point I commence to grow a trifle nervous, for

while she is obviously expectin' me to continue in my oration, I have run out of instructions to reiterate.

". . . And . . . ummm . . ." I sez, tryin' to think of what I have overlooked.

". . . And not to start any trouble!" she finishes, lookin' at me hard-like. "Right?"

"Yeah. Sure, Bunny."

"Say it!"

". . . And not to start any trouble."

Now I am more than a little hurt that Bunny feels it is necessary to bring this point to my attention so forceful like, as in my opinion it is not in my nature to start trouble under any circumstances. Both Nunzio and me go out of our way to avoid any unnecessary disputes of a violent nature, and only bestir ourselves to bring such difficulties to a halt once they are thrust upon us. I do not, however, bring my injured feelings to Bunny's attention as I know she is a swell person who would not deliberately inflict such wounds upon the self-image of a delicate person such as myself. She is merely nervous as to the successful completion of the pending job, as I have previously orated, and would only feel bad if I were to let on how callous and heartless she was behavin'. There are many in my line of work who display similar signs of nervousness when preparin' for a major assignment. I once worked with a guy what had a tendency to fidget with a sharp knife when waitin' for a job to commence, usually on the bods of his fellow caperers. One can only be understandin' of the motivationals of such types and not take offense at their personal foibles when the heat is on. This is one of the secrets of success learned early on by us executive types. Be that as it may, I am forced to admit I am more than a little relieved when it

is time for the job to begin, allowin' me to part company
with Bunny for a while.

As a worker type, I report to work much earlier than
is required for office types like Bunny. Why this is I am
not sure, but it is one of those inescapable inequities with
which life is fraught . . . like your line always bein' the
longest when they are broken down by alphabet.

To prepare for my undercover maneuverin's, I have
abandoned my normally spiffy threads in order to dress
more appropriate for the worker types with which I am
to intermingle. This is the only part of the assignment
which causes me any discomfort. You see, the more successful a worker type is, the more he dresses like a
skid-row bum or a rag heap, so that he looks like he is
either ready to roll in the mud or has just been rolled
himself, which is in direct contradiction to what I learned
in business college.

For those of you to whom this last tidbit of knowledge
comes as a surprise, I would hasten to point out that I
have indeed attended higher learnin' institutes, as that is
the only way to obtain the master's type degree that I
possess. If perchance you wonder, as some do, why a
person with such credentials should choose the line of
work that I have to pursue, my reasons are twofold:
Firstus, I am a social type who perfers workin' with
people; and second, I find my sensitive nature is repelled
by the ruthlessness necessitated by bein' an upper management type. I simply do not have it in me to mess up
people's lives with layoffs and plant shut-downs and the
like. Rather, I find it far more sociable to break an occasional leg or two or perhaps rearrange a face a little than
to live with the more long-term damage inflicted by upper
management for the good of their respective companies.
Therefore, as I am indeed presented with the enviable

position of havin' a choice in career paths, I have traditionally opted to be an order taker rather than an order giver. It's a cleaner way to make a livin'.

So anyway, I reports for work bright and early and am shown around the plant before commencin' my actual duties. Let me tell you I am impressed by this set-up like I have seldom been impressed by nothin' before. It is like Santa's North Pole elf sweatshop done up proper.

When I was in grad school, I used to read a lot of comics. Most particularly I was taken by the ads they used to carry therein for X-Ray Glasses and Whoopie Cushions and such, which I was unfortunately never able to afford as I was not an untypical student and therefore had less money than your average eight-year-old. Walkin' into the plant, however, I suddenly realized that this particular set of indulgences had not truly passed me by as I had feared.

The place was gargantuous, by which I mean it was really big, and jammed from wall to wall to ceilin' with conveyor belts and vats and stacks of materials and boxes labeled in languages I am not privileged to recognize, as well as large numbers of worker types strollin' around checkin' gauges and pushin' carts and otherwise engaged in the sorts of activities one does when the doors are open and there's a chance that the management types might come by on their way to the coffee machine and look in to see what they're doin'. What was even more impressive was the goods in production. At a glance I could see that as an admirer of cheap junk gimmicks, I had indeed died and gone to pig heaven. It was my guess, however uneducated, that what I had found was the major supplier for those ads which I earlier referenced, as well as most of the peddlers in the Bazaar who cater to the tourist trade.

Now right away I can see what the problem is, as most of the goods bein' produced are a small and portable nature, and who could resist waltzin' off with a few samples in their pockets? Merchandise of this nature would be enough to tempt a saint, of which I seriously doubt the majority of the work force is made up of.

At the time I think that this will make my job substantially easier than anticipated. It is my reasonin' that all I need do is figure out how I myself would liberate a few choice items, then watch to see who is doin' the same. Of course, I figure it will behoove me to test my proposed system myself so as to see if it really can be done in such a manner, and at the same time acquire a little bonus or two I can gloat about in front of Nunzio.

First, however, I had to concentrate on establishin' myself as a good worker so that no one would suspect that I was there for anythin' else other than makin' an honest wage.

The job I was assigned to first was simple enough for a person of my skills and dexterity. All I had to do was sprinkle a dab of Pixie Dust on each Magic Floating Coaster as it came down the line. The major challenge seemed to be to be sure to apply as little as possible, as Pixie Dust is expensive even at bulk rates and one definitely does not want to give the customer more than they paid for.

With this in mind, I set to work . . . only to discover that the job was actually far more complex than I had originally perceived. You see, the Pixie Dust is kept in a large bag, which floats because that is what the Pixie Dust within does. The first trick is to keep the bag from floatin' away while one is workin' with it, which is actually harder than it sounds because the Pixie Dust is almost strong enough to float the bag *and* whoever is attemptin' to hold it down. There is a safety line attached to the bag as an anchor, but it holds the bag too high to work with. Consequently one must wrestle with the bag while applyin' the Pixie Dust, a feat which is not unlike tryin' to hold a large beach ball under water while doin' needlepoint, and only rely on the safety line to haul the bag down into position again should it get away, which it often does. One might ask whyfore the line is not made shorter to hold the bag in the proper position and thereby make the job simpler. I suppose it is the same reason that working-type mothers will drown their children at birth if they feel there is the slightest chance they will grow up to be production engineers.

The other problem I encountered was one which I am surprised no one saw to fit to warn me about. That is that when one works with Pixie Dust, it must be remembered that it floats, and therefore pours up instead of down.

When first I attempted to sprinkle a little Pixie Dust on a Magic Floating Coaster, I was puzzled as to why the coaster would not subsequently float. On the chance that I had not applied a sufficient quantity of the substance in question, I added some more . . . and then a little more, not realizin' that it was floatin' up toward the ceilin' instead of down onto the coaster. Unfortunately, I was bent over the coaster at the time, as I was tryin' to keep the bag from floatin' away, and unbeknownst to me the dust was sprinklin' onto me rather than the coaster in question. The first admissible evidence I had that things was goin' awry was when I noticed that my feet were no longer in contact with the floor and that indeed I had become as buoyant as the bag which I was tryin' to hold down. Fortuitously, my grip is firm enough to crumble bricks so I managed to maintain my hold on the bag and eventually pull myself down the safety line instead of floatin' to the ceilin' in independent flight. Further, I was able to brush the Pixie Dust off my clothes so as to maintain my groundward orientation as well as my dignity.

The only thing which was not understandable about this passing incident was the uninvolvement of the other worker types. Not only had they not come over to assist me in my moment of misfortune, they had also refrained from making rude and uproarious noises at my predicament. This second point in particular I concerned myself with as bein' unusual, as worker types are notorious jokesters and unlikely to pass up such an obvious opportunity for low amusement.

The reason for this did indeed beome crystalline when we finally broke for lunch.

I was just settlin' in to enjoy my midday repast, and chanced to ask the worker type seated next to me to pass me a napkin from the receptice by him as it was not within my reach. Instead of goin' along with this request as one would expect any civilized person to do, this joker mouths off to the effect that he won't give the time of day to any company spy, much less a napkin. Now if there is one thing I will not tolerate it is bein' called a fink, especially when I happen to be workin' as one. I therefore deem it necessary to show this individual the error of his assumptions by bendin' him a little in my most calm, friendly manner. Just when I think we are startin' to communicate, I notice that someone is beatin' me across the back with a chair. This does nothin' to improve my mood, as I am already annoyed to begin with, so I prop the Mouth against a nearby wall with one hand, thereby freein' the other which I then use to snag the other cretin as he winds up for another swing. I am just beginnin' to warm up to my work when I hear a low whistle of warnin' from the crowd which has naturally gathered to watch our discussion, and I look around to see one of the foremen ambling over to see what the commotion's about.

Now foremen are perhaps the lowest form of management, as they are usually turncoat worker types, and this one proves to be no exception to the norm. Without so much as a how-do-you-do, he commences to demand to know what's goin' on and who started it anyway. As has been noted, I already had my wind up and was seriously considerin' whether or not to simply expand our discussion group to include the foreman when I remember how nervous Bunny was and consider the difficulty I would have explainin' the situation to her if I were to suffer termination the first day on the job for roughin' up a management type. Consequently I shift my grip from my two dance partners to my temper and proceed to explain to the foreman that no one has started anythin' as indeed nothin' is happenin' . . . that my colleagues chanced to fall down and I was simply helpin' them to their feet is all.

My explanations can be very convincing, as any jury can tell you, and the foreman decides to accept this one without question, somehow overlookin' the fact that I had helped the Mouth to his feet with such enthusiasm that his feet were not touchin' the floor when the proceedin's were halted. Perhaps he attributed this phenomenon to the Pixie Dust which was so fond of levitatin' anything in the plant that wasn't tied down. Whatever the reason, he buys the story and wanders off, leavin' me to share my lunch with my two colleagues whose lunch has somehow gotten tromped on during playtime.

Apparently, my display of masculine-type prowess has convinced everyone that I am indeed not a company spy, for the two guys which jumped me in such an unprofessional manner is now very eager to chat on the friendliest of terms. The one I have been referrin' to as the Mouth turns out to be named Roxie, and his chairswingin' buddy is Sion. Right away we hit it off as they seem to be regular-type guys, even if they can't throw a punch to save their own skins, and it seems we share a lot of common interests . . . like skirts and an occasional bet on the ponies. Of course, they are immediately advanced to the top of my list of suspects, as anyone who thinks like me is also likely to have little regard for respectin' the privacy rights of other people's property.

The other thing they tell me before we return to our respective tasks is that the Pixie Dust job I am doin' is really a chump chore reserved for new worker types what don't know enough to argue with their assignments. It is suggested that I have a few words with the foreman, as he has obviously been impressed with my demeanor, and see if I can't get some work more in keepin' with my obvious talents. I am naturally grateful for this advice, and pursue their suggestion without further delay.

The foreman does indeed listen to my words, and sends me off to a new station for the balance of the day. Upon arrivin' at the scene of my reassignment, however, it occurs to me that perhaps I would have been wiser to keep my big yap in a closed position.

My new job really stinks . . . and I mean to tell you this is meant as literal as possible. All I had to do, see, was stand at the end of a conveyor belt and inspect the end product as it came off the line. Now, when I say "end product," this is also meant to be interpretated very literal-like. The quicker of you have doubtlessly perceived by now the product to which I am referrin', but for the benefit of the slower readers and sober editors, I will clarify my allusions.

What I am inspectin' is rubber Doggie Doodle, which comes in three sizes: Embarrassing, Disgusting, and Unbelievable. This is not, of course, how they are labeled, but rather how I choose to refer to them after a mere few moments' exposure. Now since, as I have mentioned before, this is a class operation, it is to be expected that our product has to be noticeably different than similar offerin's on the market. It is unfortunate that as the Final Inspector, I must deal with the finished product, which means before it goes into the boxes, but after the "Realistic, Life-like Aroma that Actually Sticks to Your Hands" is added.

It is also unfortunate that I am unable to locate either the foreman or the two jokers who had advised me for the rest of the afternoon. Of course, I am not permitted the luxury of a prolonged search, as the conveyor belt continues to move whether the inspector is inspectin' or not, and in no time at all the work begins to pile up. As I am not particularly handy with a shovel, I deem it wisest to continue workin' and save our discussion for a later, more private time.

Now mind you, the work doesn't really bother me all that much. One of the chores me and Nunzio toss coins over back home is cleanin' up after the Boss's dragon, and after that, Doggie Doodle really looks like a bit of an understatement, if you know what I mean. If anything, this causes me to chuckle a bit as I work, for while I am on assignment Nunzio must do the honors all by himself, so by comparison my end of the stick looks pretty clean. Then too, the fact that Roxie and Sion is now playin' tricks on me is a sign that I am indeed bein' accepted as one of the worker types, which will make my job considerably easier.

The only real problem I have with my assignment is that, considerin' the product with which I am workin', I feel it would be unwise to test the security-type precautions when I leave work that night. Even if I wished to liberate a few samples, which I was not particularly desirous of doin' since as I have noted we already have lots at home of a far superior quality, the "Realistic, Life-like Aroma that Really Sticks to Your Hands," would negate its passin' unnoticed by even the densest security-type guard.

As it turns out, this was a blessin' incognito. When closin' time finally rolls around, I discover that it would not be as easy to sneak stuff out of this plant as I had originally perceived. Everything the worker types took out of the plant with 'em was given the once and twice over by hard-eyed types who definitely knew what they were doin', and while we didn't have to go through a strip search, we did have to walk one at a time through a series of alarm systems that used a variety of rays to frisk us for objects and substances belongin' to the company. As it was, I almost got into trouble because there were still lingerin' specks of Pixie Dust on me from my mornin' duties, but Roxie stepped forward and explained things to the guards that was rapidly gatherin' and they settled for reclaimin' the Pixie Dust without things gettin' too personal.

This settled things between me and Roxie for the Doggie Doodle joke, and after I bounced Sion against the wall a few times to show my appreciation for his part in the prank, we all went off in search of some unprintable diversions.

Now if this last bit seems, perchance, a little shallow

to you, you must first consider the whole situational before renderin' your verdict. I think it's been referenced before that the factory under investigation is located in one of those unlisted dimensions the Deveels specialize in. As the only way into this dimension from the Bazaar is through the owner's front-type operation, and as he is not wild about the notion of hundreds of worker types traipsin' through his office each shift, part of the contract for workin' in said factory is that one has to agree to stay in this unlisted dimension for a week at a time. To this end, the owner has provided rooms for the worker types, but as he is cheap even for a Deveel, each room is shared by bein's workin' different shifts. That is to say, you only have your room for one shift, and the rest of the time you're either workin' or hangin' out. Just so's we don't get bored between workin' and sleepin', the owner has also provided a variety of bars, restaurants, movies, and video joints for our amusement, all of which cost but can be charged back against our paychecks. If this seems like a bit of a closed economy to you, I would hasten to remind you that no one has ever accused the Deveels of bein' dumb when it comes to turnin' a profit. Anyway, all of this is to explain why it is that I am forced to go carousin' with Roxie and Sion instead of retirin' to my room to re-read the classics as would be my normal bent.

Now to be truthful with you, this carryin' on is not nearly so bad as I am lettin' on. It is simply that it is embarrassin' to my carefully maintained image to admit how really dull these evenings was, so's I reflexively sort of try to build them up more than I should. I mean, you'd think that off hours with a bunch of guys what work at a magic joke and novelty factory would be a barrel of laughs. You know, more fun than callin' in

phony heist tips to the cops. Well, they surprised me by
contentin' themselves to drinkin' and gamblin' and
maybe a fistfight or two for their amusements . . . like
I say, the same old borin' stuff any good-natured bunch
of guys does. Mostly what they do is sit around and gripe
about the work at the plant and how underpaid they are
. . . which I do not pay much attention to as there is not
a worker type alive that does not indulge in this particular
pastime. In no time flat I determines that nobody in the
work force is well enough versed in the finer points of
non-backer entrepreneurmanship, which is to say crime,
to converse with me on my own level. This is not surprisin' in the age of specialization, but it does mean I don't
get nobody to talk to.

What I am gettin', though, is depressed . . . a feelin'
which continues to grow as the week rolls on. It is not
the work or the company of the worker types which is
erodin' at my morale, but rather the diminishin' possibility of puttin' a wrap on this job.

It seems the more I observe in my undercover-type
investigation, the more puzzled I become as to how the
pilferage is bein' accomplished. The better I get to know
my fellow worker types, the more I am convinced that
they are not involved in any such goin's on, even in a
marginal manner. This is not to say that they are lackin'
in the smarts department, as they are easily as quick on
the uptake as anyone I ever worked with in school or the
business. Rather, I am makin' a tribute to the tightness
of the plant security which must necessarily be penetrated
in order to perpetrate such an activity.

As I have earlier said, this is an age of specialization,
and none of the worker types I meet have adequately
applied themselves to be able to hold a candle to me in
my particular field of endeavor. Now realizin' that after

a week of intense schemin', I have not yet come up with a plan for samplin' the merchandise that I feel has enough of a chance of succeedin' as to make it worthwhile to try, I cannot convince myself that the security can be cracked by any amateur, however talented.

Considerin' this, I am edgin' closer to the unpleasant conclusion that not only is it long odds against us findin' a fast answer, there is a chance we might not be able to crack this case at all. Such thoughts cause me great anxieties, which lead to depression as I am as success-oriented as the next person.

My mood truly bottoms out at the end of the week, specifically when I am presented with my paycheck. Now, I am not countin' on the money I earn as a worker type, as I am already bein' well subsidized by the Boss. Nonetheless I am surprised to see the amount my week's worth of toil has actually brought me. To be truthful, I have again yielded to the temptation of understatement. I was not surprised, I was shocked . . . which is not a good thing for, as anyone in the Mob can tell you, when I am shocked I tend to express the unsettlement of my nerves physically.

The fact that I am not needin' the money in question means that I was only a little shocked, so it only took three of my fellow worker types to pull me off the payroll type what slipped me the bad news. Of course, by that time I had also been hit by a couple of tranquilizer darts which I am told is standard issue for most companies in the Bazaar to ease personnel relations. If, perchance, your company does not already follow this policy, I heartily give it my recommend, as it certainly saves depreciation on your payroll types and therefore minimizes the expense of trainin' new ones.

Anyway, once I am calmed down to a point where I

am merely tossin' furniture and the payroll type has re-composed himself, which is to say he has received suf-ficient first aid to talk, he explains the realities of life to me. Not only has the cost of the aforementioned carousin' been deducted from my earnin's, but also charges for my room which, realizin' the figure quoted only repre-sents a third of the take on that facility, puts it several notches above the poshest resort it has ever been my decadent pleasure to patronize. Also there is an itemized bill for every bit or scrap of waste that has occurred at my duty station durin' the week, down to the last speck of Pixie Dust. Normally I would be curious as to how this accountin' was done, as it indicates a work force in the plant even more efficient than the security types which have been keepin' me at bay, but at the time I was too busy bein' outraged at bein' charged retail instead of cost for the materials lost.

All that keeps me from truly expressin' my opinion of the situation is that Roxie explains that I am not bein' singled out for special treatment, but that this is indeed a plant-wide policy which all the worker types must suf-fer. He also points out that the cost of the first aid for the payroll type is gonna be charged against my paycheck, and that what I have left will not be sufficient for me to indulge myself in another go 'round.

Thus it is that I am doubly disheartened when I hook up with Bunny for our weekly meetin' and debriefin', bein' as how I am not only a failure but a poor failure which is the worst kind to be.

"Guido, what's wrong?" she sez when we meet. "You look terrible!"

As I have said, Bunny is a swell head, but she is still a skirt, which means she has an unerring instinct for what to say to pick a guy up when he's under the weather.

"I am depressed," I sez, since she wasn't around when I explained it to you. "The workin' conditions at the plant are terrible, especially considerin' the pay we aren't gettin'."

At this, Bunny rolls her eyes and groans to express her sympathy.

"Oh, Guido! You're talking just like a . . . what is it that you call them? Oh, yes. Just like a worker type."

"That's 'cause I *am* a worker type!"

This earns me the hairy eyeball.

"No, you're not," she sez real hard-like. "You're an executive for M.Y.T.H. Inc. here on an investigation. Now quit being negative and let's talk about the job."

It occurs to me that she has a truly unusual concept of how to avoid negative thinkin'.

"Suit yourself," I sez, givin' her my best careless shrug like I usually save for court performances. "As far as the job goes, I am truly at a dead end. After a week I have discovered nothin' and don't have the foggiest where to look next."

"Good!" she sez, breakin' into a smile which could melt an iceberg, of which there are very few at the Bazaar with which I could test my hyperbole. Naturally I am surprised.

"Perhaps my small-but-normally-accurate ears are deceivin' me, Bunny. Did I understand you to say that it's a good thing that I am gettin' nowhere in my investigations?"

"That's right. You see, I think I'm on to something at my end, and if you're coming up empty in the plant, maybe you can help me with my theories! Now here's what I want you to do."

Followin' Bunny's suggestion, I start out the next week

by bracin' the foreman to reassign me to work in the warehouse on inventory. At first he is reluctant as he does not like worker types tellin' him his job, but after I point out to him how small the hospitalization benefits provided by the owner really are, he becomes far more reasonable.

All I have to do to give Bunny the support she requests is to double-check the materials comin' into the plant, and send her an extra copy of each day's tally in the inter-office mail. This pleases me immensely, as it is not only easy work, it also gives me substantial amounts of free time with which I can pursue a project of my own.

You see, I am still more than a little steamed over the hatchet job which was performed upon my paycheck. I therefore take it upon myself to commence conductin' my own unofficial survey as to workin' conditions around the plant, and since my eye has the benefit of business school trainin', which most of the workin' types have not bothered with, it becomes rapidly apparent that the situational stinks worse than the Doggie Doodle did.

Just as an example, the plant has made a practice of hirin' all sorts of bein's, many of which is extremely difficult to describe without gettin' vulgar. Now this is not surprisin' considerin' the Bazaar is the main source for their recruitin', but it makes for some teeth-grindin' inequalities in the pay scales.

Before the wrong idea is given, let me elucidate for a moment on the point of view I am comin' from. I personally don't care much who or what is workin' next to me as long as they can carry their share of the job. You will notice I have not even mentioned that Roxie is bright orange and Sion is mauve, as I feel this has nothin' to do with my assessment of their personalities or their abilities. I will admit to bein' a little uneasy around bein's what got more arms or legs than I do, but this is more a professional reaction, since should the occasion arise that we might have a difference of opinion, my fightin' style is intended for opposition what can throw the same number of punches and kicks per side as I can, and a few extra fists can make a big difference. But, as I say, this is more a professional wariness than any judgment on their overall worth as bein's. I only mention this on the off chance that some of my remarks about strange bein's might be taken as bein' pergerdous, a rap of which I have never been convicted. I am not that sort of person.

As I was sayin', though, the plant has lots of strange bein's workin' the line. The indignity of the situation, however, is that even though they got these extra arms and in some cases is doin' the work of several worker types, they is gettin' paid the same as anyone else. While to some this might seem unfair to the ones bein' so exploited, I see it as a threat to the worker types with the usual count of arms and legs, as it will obviously save the company significant cost if they can hire as many of the former as possible, whilst layin' off a dispro-portionate number of the latter.

Another inequality I observe concerns the security types which I have been unable to circumvent. Now this has been a source of curiosity to me since I first arrived at the plant, since it doesn't take an accountin' whiz to figure out that if the plant is payin' the security types what they're worth, their cost should be substantially more than would seem economically wise. I chance across the answer one time when I happen to eavesdrop on a couple off-duty lunchin' security types who are gripin' about their jobs. It seems that they are underpaid as much as us workin' types, despite the fact that they are safeguardin' stuff worth millions! While this is

doubtlessly unfair, I do not include it in my notes because
I have found that it is not only not unusual, but is actually
customary for plants or societies to underpay their guardian types. I suppose that as bonkers as it seems, this is
in actuality the way things should be. If guardian types
made a decent wage, then criminal types like me would
go into that line of work as it has better hours and better
retirement benefits than the career path I am currently
pursuin', and if there was no crime there would be no
need for guardian types and we would all end up unemployed. Viewin' it that way, the status quo is probably
for the best.

Anyway, I continues to keep my eyes and ears open
until I feel I have gathered sufficient injustices to make
my point, then I wait for the right moment to present my
findin's. This proves to be no great test of my patience,
since, as I have noted, the worker types love to gripe
about their jobs and tonight proves to be no exception
to this rule.

"What do you think, Guido?" Roxie sez, turnin' to
me. "Do the guys workin' the Dribble Toilets have it
worse than the ones workin' the Battery-Operated
Whoopie Cushions?"

I make a big show of thinkin' hard before I give my
answer.

"I think," I sez carefully, "that if brains was dyna-
mite, the whole plant wouldn't have the powder to blow
its nose."

It takes him a minute to get my drift, but when he
does, his eyes go real mean.

"What's that supposed to mean?"

"I mean I've been sittin' here listenin' to you guys
bellyache for nearly two weeks now, and ain't none of
youse heard a thing that's goin' on."

"All right, Mr. Doggie Doodle, if you're so smart why don't you tell all of us who have been workin' here for years what it is you've learned in a whole two weeks."

I choose to ignore the Doggie Doodle crack, as there are now several tables of worker types listenin' to our conversation and I'm afraid I'll lose their attention if I take the time to bust Roxie's head.

"Youse guys spend all your time arguin' about who's gettin' honked the worst, and in the meantime you're missin' the point. The point is that you're *all* gettin' the Purple Shaft."

With that I commences to itemize a dozen or so of the more reprehensible examples of the exploitation of worker types I have noted in my investigation. By the time I am done, the whole bar is listenin', and there is an ugly murmur goin' around.

"All right, Guido. You've made your point," Roxie sez, tryin' to take another swallow of his drink before he realizes that it's empty. "So what are we supposed to do about it? We don't set company policy."

I shows him the smile that makes witnesses lose their memories.

"We don't set company policy, but we *do* decide whether or not we're gonna work for the wages offered in the conditions provided."

At this, Roxie lights up like he just won the lottery.

"That's right!" he sez. "They control the plant, but without us workers there won't be no Doggie Doodle to ship!"

The crowd is gettin' pretty worked up now, and there's a lot of drink buyin' and back slappin' goin' on when someone just has to raise a discouragin' word.

"So what's to stop 'em from just hiring a new work force if we hold out?"

That is Sion talkin'. As you may have noticed, he don't mouth off near as much as Roxie does, but when he opens up, the other worker types are inclined to listen. This time is no exception, and the room starts to quiet down as the worker types try to focus on this new problem.

"C'mon, Sion," Roxie sez, tryin' to laugh it off. "What idiots would work for these wages under these conditions?"

"Roxie, *we've* been doing just that for years! I don't think they'll have any more trouble finding a new work force than they had finding the old one."

I decided it was time I took a hand in the proceedin's.

"There are a few things you are overlookin', Sion," I sez. "First off, it will take time to hire and train a new work force, and durin' that time the plant ain't producin' Doggie Doodle to sell, which means the owner is losin' money which he does not like to do."

Sion just shrugged at that one.

"True enough, but he'd probably rather take the short-term loss of a shutdown than the long-term expense of giving us higher wages."

"Which brings up the other thing you're overlookin'."

"Which is?"

"There is one intolerable workin' condition a new work force would have to endure that we haven't . . . to wit, us! We don't have to get past us to come to work each mornin', and whilst the security types are aces at guardin' a plant, it is my best appraisal that they would not be able to provide bodyguard service for an entire new work force."

This seemed to satisfy the objection in question, and we then got down to workin' out the details, for while from the outside it may seem simple to organize a labor movement, there is much to be planned before anythin' can actually be set into motion. The other two shifts had to be brought on board and a list of demands agreed upon, not to mention the buildin' of a contingency fund in case the other side wanted to try starvin' us out.

A lot of the guys wanted me to run the thing, but I felt I could not accept in clear consciousness and successfully proposed Roxie for the position. The alibi I gave is that the worker types should be represented by someone who has more than two weeks' experience on the job, but in reality I wasn't sure how much longer I had before the Boss pulled me back to my normal duties and I did not want the movement to flounder from havin' its leader disappear sudden like. The chore I did volunteer for was givin' lessons in how to handle any outsiders the plant tried to hire, as most of the current worker types did not know a sawed-off pool cue from a tire iron when it came to labor negotiations.

Between workin' in the warehouse and helpin' with the movement, I was so busy I almost missed my weekly meetin' with Bunny. Fortuitously I remembered, which is a good thing as Bunny is a doll and no doll likes to be forgotten.

"Hi, Babe!" I sez, givin' her one of my seediest winks. "How's it goin'?"

"Well, you're sure in a chipper mood," she sez, grinnin' back at me. "I thought I'd have good news for you, but I guess you already heard."

"Heard? Heard what?"

"The assignment's over. I've cracked the case."

Now this causes me a little guilt and embarrassment, as I have not thought about our assignment for days, but

I cover for it by actin' enthusiastic instead.

"No foolin'? You found out how the stuff is bein' liberated?"

"Well, actually it turns out to be a case of embezzlement, not pilferage. One of the Deveels in Accounting was tinkering with the receiving records and paying for more than was coming in at the shipping dock."

"Bunny," I sez, "try to remember that my degree is not in accounting. Could you perhaps try to enlighten me in baby talk so's I can understand the nature of the heist?"

"Okay. When we buy the raw materials, each shipment is counted and a tally sent to Accounting. That tally determines how much we pay our supplier, as well as alerting us as to how much raw material there is in inventory. Now our embezzler had a deal going with the suppliers to bill us for more material than we actually received. He would rig the receiving tallies to tie out to the overage, pay the supplier for goods they never shipped, then split the extra money with them. The trouble was that since the same numbers were used for the inventories, the records showed that there were more goods in inventory than were actually there, so when the plant came up short, the owner thought the employees were stealing from him. The missing goods weren't being pilfered, they were never in the plant at all!"

I gave a low whistle of appreciation.

"That's great, Bunny! The Boss'll be real proud of you when he hears."

That actually made her blush a little.

"I didn't do it all by myself, you know. I wouldn't have been able to prove anything if you hadn't been feeding me duplicate records on the side."

"A mere trifling," I sez expansively. "I for one am

goin' to make sure the Boss knows just what a gem he has workin' for him so's you get your just esteem in his eyes.''

"Thanks, Guido,'' she sez, layin' a hand on my arm. "I try to impress him, but sometimes I think . . .''

She breaks off and looks away, and it occurs to me that she is about to commence leakin' at the eyes. In an effort to avert this occurrence which will undoubtedly embarrass us both, I wrench the conversation back to our original topic.

"So what are they goin' to do with this bum now that you caught him?''

"Nothing.''

"Say what?''

"No, that's not right. He's going to get a promotion.''

"Get outta here!''

She turns back, and I can see she's now got an impish grin on, which is a welcome change.

"Really. It turns out he's the owner's brother-in-law. The owner is so impressed with the smarts it took to set up this scam that he's giving the little creep a higher position in the organization. I guess he wants him stealing for the company instead of from it.''

It takes me several moments to realize that my normally agile mouth is stuck in the open position.

"So where does that leave us?'' I manage at last.

"With a successful investigation under our belts along with a fat bonus for resolving the thing so fast. I've got a hunch, though, that part of that bonus is gag money to ensure we don't spread it around that the owner was being flimflammed by his own brother-in-law.''

Now I am indeed glad that we have resolved the pilfer-age assignment without implicatin' any of the worker types I have been buddies with, but at the same time I

am realizin' that with the job over, I will not be around
to help them out when the Doggie Doodle hits the fan.

"Well, that's that, I guess. We'd better report in to
the Boss and see what's been happenin' while we've
been gone."

"Is something wrong, Guido? You seem a little
down."

"Aaah! It's nothin', Bunny. Just thinkin' that I'll miss
some of the guys back at the plant, is all."

"Maybe not," she sez, real mysterious like.

Now it's my turn to give her the hairy eyeball.

"Now, Bunny," I sez, "if you've got sumpin' up
your sleeve other than lint, I would suggest you share it
with me. You know I am not good when it comes to
surprises."

"Well, I was going to wait until we got back home,
but I suppose it won't hurt to give you a preview."

She looks around like there might be someone listenin'
in, then hunches forward so I can hear her whisper.

"I picked up a rumor back at the plant office that there
may be a union forming at the magic factory. I'm going
to suggest to Skeeve that we do a little prospecting . . .
you know, put in a bid. Can you imagine what we could
charge for breaking up a union?"

I develop a sudden interest in the ceiling.

"Uh, Bunny?" I sez. "I know you want to impress
the Boss with how good you are at findin' work for us,
but I think in the longer run that it would be in the best
interests of M.Y.T.H. Inc. to pass on this particular
caper."

"But why? The owner stands to lose ten times as much
if a union forms than he was dropping to embezzlement.
We could make a real killing here. He already knows
our work."

In response, I lean back and give her a slow smile.

"When it comes to makin' a killin', Bunny, I would advise you not to try to teach your grandmother, which in this case is me, how to steal sheep. Furthermore, there are times when it is wisest not to let the client know too much about your work . . . and trust me, Bunny, this is one such time!"

Chapter Two:

"It all hinges on your definition of 'a good time'!"
—L. BORGIA

. . .AN OUTSIDE AGITATOR and a union organizer! And
to think I was paying him to slit my throat!!''

I somehow managed to keep a straight face, which
was harder than it sounds.

''Actually, Mr. Bane, I was paying him to help uncover
the source of your inventory leak, which he did, and you
were paying him to work in your factory, which he also
did. I'm not sure exactly what it is that you're complaining about.''

For a moment I thought the Deveel was going to come
across the desk at my throat.

''What I'm complaining about is that your so-called
agent organized a union in my factory that's costing me
a bundle!''

''There's no proof he was involved . . . .''

''So how come his name comes up every time . . . .''

''. . . And even if he was, I'm not sure what concern
it is of mine. I run a business, Mr. Bane, with employees,

37

not slaves. What they do on their off hours is their affair, not mine.''

"But he was acting as your agent!!!''

". . . To investigate the pilferage problem, which, I'm told, has been settled.''

As we were speaking, Chumley poked his head into my office, saw what was going on, and came in all the way, shifting to his big bad troll persona as he did. In case you are wondering, I was working without a receptionist at the time, having deemed it wise to have both Bunny and Guido lie low for a while after finding out what had *really* happened on their last assignment. As an additional precaution, I had insisted that they hide out separately, since I was afraid that Bunny would kill Guido if they were alone within an arm's reach of each other. For some reason my secretary seemed to take Guido's labor activities very personally.

". . . Now, if you'll excuse me, Mr. Bane, I'm rather busy at the moment. If you wish to pursue the matter further, I suggest you take it up with Big Crunch here. He usually handles the complaints for our company.''

The Deveel started to speak angrily as he glanced behind him, then did a double-take and swallowed whatever it was he was about to say as his gaze went up . . . and up! As I can testify from firsthand experience, trolls can look very large when viewed from up close.

"Little Deveel want to fight with Big Crunch? Crunch likes to fight!''

Bane pinked slightly, then turned back to me.

"Now look, Sk . . . Mr. Skeeve. All that's in the past, right? What say we talk about what your outfit can do to help me with this labor thing.''

I leaned back in my chair and put my hand behind my head.

"Not interested, Mr. Bane. Labor disputes are not our forte. If you'd like a little free advice, though, I'd advise you to settle. Prolonged strikes can be very costly."

The Deveel started to bare his teeth, then glanced at Chumley again and twisted it into a smile. In fact, he didn't say another word until he reached the door, and even then he spoke with careful respect.

"Um . . . if it ain't asking too much, could you send this Guido around, just to say hi to the workers? What with him disappearing the way he did, there are some who are saying that I had him terminated. It might make things a little easier for me in the negotiations."

"I'll ask him . . . next time I see him."

The Deveel nodded his thanks and left.

"Bit of a sticky wicket, eh, Skeeve?" Chumley said, relaxing back into his normal self.

"Just another satisfied customer of M.Y.T.H. Inc. stopping by to express his gratitude," I sighed. "Remind me not to send Guido out on assignment again without *very* explicit instructions. Hmmmm?"

"How about a muzzle and leash?"

I shook my head and sat forward in my chair again, glancing over the paperwork that seemed to breed on my desk whenever Bunny was away.

"Enough of that. What can I do for you, Chumley?"

"Hmm? Oh, nothing, really. I was just looking for little sister to see if she wanted to join me for lunch. Has she been about?"

"Tananda? As a matter of fact, I just sent her out on an assignment. Sorry."

"No matter. What kind of work are you giving the old girl, anyway?"

"Oh, nothing big," I said, rummaging through the paper for the letter I had been reading when Bane burst in. "Just a little collection job a few dimensions over."

"ARE YOU OUT OF YOUR BLOODY MIND??!!!"

Chumley was suddenly leaning over my desk, his two moon eyes of different sizes scant inches from my own. It occurred to me that I had never seen the troll really angry. Upon viewing it, I sincerely hoped I would never see it again. That is, of course, assuming I could survive the first time.

"Whoa! Chumley! Calm! What's wrong?"

"YOU SENT HER OUT ON A COLLECTION JOB ALONE?"

"She should be all right," I said hastily. "It sounded like a pretty calm mission. In fact, that's why I sent her instead of one of our heavy hitters . . . I thought the job called for finesse, not muscle. Besides, Tananda can take care of herself pretty well."

The troll groaned and let his head fall forward until it thudded on my desk. He stayed that way for a few moments, breathing deeply, before he spoke.

"Skeeve . . . Skeeve . . . Skeeve. I keep forgetting how new you are to our little family."

This was starting to get me worried.

"C'mon, Chumley, what's wrong? Tananda will be okay, won't she?"

The troll raised his head to look at me.

"Skeeve, you don't realize . . . we all relax around you, but you never see us when you aren't around."

Terrific.

"Look, Chumley. Your logic is as enviable as ever, but can't you just say what the problem is? If you think Tananda's in danger . . ."

"SHE'S NOT THE ONE I'M WORRIED ABOUT!"

With visible effort, Chumley composed himself.

"Skeeve . . . let me try to explain. Little sister is a wonderful person, and I truly love and admire her, but she has a tendency to . . . overreact under pressure. Mum always said it was her competitive reaction to having an older brother who could tear things apart without trying, but some of the people she's worked with tend to simply describe it as a mean streak. In a nutshell, though, Tananda has a bigger flair for wanton destruction than I do . . . or anyone else I've ever met. Now, if this job you're describing calls for finesse . . ."

He broke off and shook his head.

"No," he said with a ring of finality to his voice. "There's no other way to handle it. I'll just have to catch up with her and try to keep her from getting too out of hand. Which dimension did you say she was headed for again?"

The direct question finally snapped me out of the mind-freeze his explanation had put me in.

"Really, Chumley. Aren't you exaggerating just a little? I mean, how much trouble could she cause?"

The troll sighed.

"Ever hear of a dimension called Rinasp?"

"Can't say that I have."

"That's because there's no one there anymore. That's the last place little sister went on a collection job."

"I've got the name of the dimension here somewhere!" I said, diving into my paperwork with newfound desperation.

Chumley's Tale

DASH IT ALL TO BLAZES anyway! You'd think by now that Skeeve would have the sense to look a bit before he leaped . . . especially when his leaping tends to involve

others as it does! If he thinks that Tananda can't . . . If
he can't figure out that even I don't . . . Well, he has
no idea of the way our Mum raised us, is all I've got to
say.

Of course, one cannot expect wonders from a Klahd
raised by a Pervert, can one . . . hmmm?? Well, Chumley
old boy, time to muddle through one more time, what?

I must admit this latest collection assignment for
Tananda had me worried. At her best little sister tends
to lack tact, and lately . . .

As near as I can tell, there was bad blood building
between her and Bunny. They had never really hit it off
well, but things had gotten noticeably sticky since Don
Bruce's niece set her cap for Skeeve. Not that little sister
had any designs on the lad herself, mind you. If anything,
her feelings toward him are more sisterly than anything
else . . . Lord help him. Rather it seems that it's Bunny's
tactics that are setting Tananda's teeth on edge.

You see, what with Bunny trying to be so spit-spot
efficient on the job to impress Skeeve, little sister has
gotten it into her head that it's making *her* look bad
professionally. Tananda has always been exceedingly
proud of her looks and her work, and what with Bunny
strutting around the office going on about how well the
last assignment went, she feels a wee bit threatened on
both counts. As near as I could tell, she was bound and
determined to prove that what she had picked up in the
Guttersnipe Survival School was more than a match for
the education Bunny had acquired at whatever finishing
school the Mob had sent her to. Combined with her
normal tendency for over-exuberance, it boded ill for
whoever it was she was out to collect from.

I was also underwhelmed by the setting for this pending
disaster. I mean, really, what kind of name is Arcadia

for a dimension? It sounds like one of those confounded video parlors. I probably would have been hard-pressed to even find it if I hadn't gotten directions along with the name. The coordinates dropped me at the edge of a town, and since they were the same ones little sister had used, I could only assume I wasn't far behind her.

At first viewing, Arcadia seemed pleasant enough; one might almost be tempted to call it quaint—the kind of quiet, sleepy place where one could relax and feel at home. For some reason, I found myself fervently hoping it would be the same when we left.

My casual inspection of the surroundings was cut short by a hail from nearby.

"Welcome to Arcadia, Stranger. Can I offer you a cool glass of juice?"

The source of this greeting was a rather gnomish old man who was perched on the seat of a tricycle vending cart. He seemed to take my appearance, both my physical makeup and my presence at this time and place, so casually I almost replied before remembering that I had a front to maintain. It's a bit of a bother, but I've found no one will hire a well-mannered troll.

"Good! Good! Crunch thirsty!"

With my best guttural growl, I grabbed two of the offered glasses and popped them in my mouth, rolling my eyes as I chewed happily. It's a good bit . . . one that seldom fails to take folks aback. The gnome, however, never batted an eye.

"Don't think I've seen you before, Stranger. What brings you to Arcadia?"

I decided to abandon any further efforts at intimidating him and instead got right to the point.

"Crunch looking for friend. Seen little woman . . . so high . . . with green hair?"

"As a matter of fact, she was just by a little bit ago. She a friend of yours?"

I nodded my head vigorously and showed my fangs.

"Crunch likes little woman. Pulled thorn from Crunch's foot once. Where little woman go?"

"Well, she asked me where the police station was, then took off in that direction . . . that way."

An awfully nice chap, really. I decided I could afford to unbend a little.

"Crunch thanks nice man. If nice man needs strong friend, call Crunch, okay?"

"Sure thing. And if I can help you any more, just give a holler."

I left then before we got too chummy. I mean, there are precious few people who will be civil, much less nice, to a troll, and I was afraid of getting more interested in continuing my conversation with him than with finding Tananda. For the good of Arcadia, that would never do.

As it was, I guess my little chat had taken longer than I had realized, for when I found Tananda she was sitting dejectedly on the steps of the police station, her business inside apparently already concluded. Things must have gone better than I had dared hope, as she was not incarcerated, and the building was still standing.

"What ho, little sister," I called, as cheerily as I could manage. "You look a little down at the mouth. Problems?"

"Oh. Hi . . . Chumley? What are you doing here?"

Fortunately, I had anticipated this question and had my answer well rehearsed.

"Just taking a bit of a holiday. I promised Aahz I would stop by this dimension and check out a few potential investments, and when Skeeve said you were here as well, I thought I would stop by and see how you were doing.''

"That can be summarized in one word," she said, resting her chin in her hands once more. "Lousy."

"Run into a spot of trouble? Come, come. Tell big brother all about it."

She gave a little shrug.

"There's not all that much to tell. I'm here on a collection assignment, so I thought I'd check with the local gendarmes to see if this guy had a record or if they knew where he was."

"And . . ." I prompted.

"Well, they know who he is all right. It seems he's a wealthy philanthropist . . . has given millions for civic improvements, helps the poor, that kind of stuff."

I scratched my head and frowned.

"Doesn't sound like the sort of chap to leave a bill unpaid, does he?"

"The real problem is going to be how to check it out. It seems he's also a bit of a recluse. No one's seen him for years."

I could see why she was depressed. It didn't sound like the kind of chore that could be finished in record time, which is, of course, what she wanted to do to make a good showing.

"Could be a bit of a sticky wicket. Who is this chap, anyway?"

"The name is Hoos. Sounds like something out of Dr. Seuss, doesn't it?"

"Actually, it sounds like a bank."

"How's that again?"

Instead of repeating myself, I simply pointed. Across the street and three doors down was a building prominently labeled Hoos National Bank.

Tananda was on her feet and moving in a flash.

"Thanks, Chumley. This may not be so bad after all."

"Don't forget. We're terribly close to the police station," I cautioned, hurrying to keep up.

"What do you mean, 'we'?" she said, stopping abruptly. "This is *my* assignment, big brother, so don't interfere or get underfoot. Capish?"

Realizing I was here to try to keep her out of trouble, I thought it ill-advised to start a brawl with Tananda in the middle of a public street, much less in front of a police station.

"Perish the thought. I just thought I'd tag along . . . as an observer. You know I love watching you work. Besides, as Mums always said, 'You can never tell when a friendly witness can come in handy.' "

I'm not sure if my words assured her, or if she simply accepted that a confirming report wouldn't hurt, but she grunted silently and headed into the bank.

The place was pretty standard for a bank: tellers' cages, tables for filling out deposit or withdrawal slips, etc. The only thing that was at all noteworthy was a special window for Inter-Dimensional Currency Exchange, which to me indicated that they did more demon business than might be expected for such an out-of-the-way dimension. I was going to point this out to Tananda, but she apparently had plans of her own. Without so much as a glance at the windows, she marched up to the manager's office.

"May I help you, Miss?" the twitty-looking fellow seated there said with a notable lack of sincerity.

"Yes. I'd like to see Mr. Hoos."

That got us a long, slow once-over with the weak eyes, his gaze lingering on me for several extra beats. I did my best to look innocent . . . which is not that easy to do for a troll.

"I'm afraid that's quite impossible," he said at last, returning his attention to the work on his desk.

I could sense Tananda fighting with her temper and mentally crossed my fingers.

"It's extremely urgent."

The eyes flicked our way again, and he set his pencil down with a visible sigh.

"Then perhaps you'd better deal with me."

"I have some information for Mr. Hoos, but I think he'd want to hear it personally."

"That's your opinion. If, after hearing it, I agree, then you might be allowed to repeat it to Mr. Hoos."

Stalemate.

Tananda seemed to recognize this as well.

"Well, I don't want to start a panic, but I have it on good authority that this bank is going to be robbed."

I was a little surprised by this, though I did my best not to show it. The bank manager, however, seemed to take it in stride.

"I'm afraid you're mistaken, young lady," he said with a tight smile.

"My sources are seldom wrong," she insisted.

"You're new to Arcadia, aren't you?"

"Well . . ."

"Once you've learned your way around, you'll realize that there isn't a criminal in the dimension who would steal from Mr. Hoos, much less try to rob his bank."

This Hoos chap was starting to sound like quite a fellow. Little sister, however, was not so easily deterred.

"What about a criminal from another dimension? Someone who isn't so impressed with Mr. Hoos?"

The manager raised an eyebrow.

"Like who, for example?"

"Well . . . what if I and my friend here decided to . . ."

That was as far as she got.

For all his stuffiness, I had to admit the manager was good. I didn't see him move or signal, but suddenly the bank was filled with armed guards. For some reason, their attention seemed to be centered on us.

I nudged Tananda, but she waved me off irritably.

". . . Of course, that was simply a 'what if.' "

"Of course," the manager smiled, without humor. "I believe our business is concluded. Good day."

"But . . ."

"I said 'Good day.' "

With that he returned to his work, ignoring us completely.

It would have been bordering on lunacy to try to take on the whole room full of guards. I was therefore startled to realize little sister was starting to contemplate that very action. As casually as I could, I started whistling Gilbert and Sullivan's "A Policeman's Lot Is Not a Happy One" as a gentle reminder of the police station not half a block away. Tananda gave me a look that would curdle cream, but she got the message and we left without further ado.

"Now what, little sister?" I said, as tactfully as I could manage.

"Isn't it obvious?"

I thought about that for a few moments.

"No," I admitted frankly. "Seems to me you've come up against a dead end."

"Then you weren't listening in there," she said, giving me one of her smug grins. "The manager gave me a big clue for where to try next.''

''. . . And that was?''

''Don't you remember he said no criminal would rob this Hoos guy?''

''Quite. So?''

''. . . So if there's a criminal connection here, I should be able to get some information out of the underworld.''

That sounded a tad ominous to me, but I have long since learned not to argue with Tananda when she gets her mind set on something. Instead, I decided to try a different approach.

''Not to be a noodge,'' I noodged, ''but how do you propose to find said underworld? They don't exactly list in the yellow pages, you know.''

Her pace slowed noticeably.

''That's a problem,'' she admitted. ''Still, there must be a way to get information around . . .''

''Can I offer you a glass of cold juice, Miss?''

It was my friend from the morning with his vending cart. A part of me wanted to wave him off, as interrupting little sister in mid-scheme is not the healthiest of pastimes, but I couldn't think of a way to do it without breaking character. Tananda surprised me, however. Instead of removing his head at the waist for breaking into her thought process, she turned her most dazzling smile on him.

''Well, hi there!'' she purred. ''Say, I never did get a chance to thank you for giving me directions to the police station this morning.''

Now, little sister's smiles can be devastating to the nervous system of anyone of the male gender, and this individual was no exception.

''Don't mention it,'' he flushed. ''If there's anything

else I can do to be of assistance . . ."

"Oh, there is one teensy-tiny favor you could do for me."

Her eyelashes fluttered like mad, and the vendor melted visibly.

"Name it."

"Wellll . . . could you tell me where I could find a hardened criminal or five? You see, I'm new here and don't know a soul I could ask."

I thought this was a little tacky and fully expected the vendor to refuse the information in a misdirected attempt to shelter the pretty girl from evil influences. The old boy seemed to take it in stride, however.

"Criminals, eh?" he said, rubbing his chin. "Haven't had much dealings with that sort for a while. When I did, though, they could usually be found down at the Suspended Sentence."

"The what?"

"The Suspended Sentence. It's a combination tavern/inn. The owner opened it after getting off a pretty sticky trial. It seems the judge wasn't wrong in letting him go, since he's gone straight, as far as I can tell, but there's a bad element that hangs out there. I think they figure some of the good luck might rub off on them."

Tananda punched me lightly in the ribs and winked.

"Well, that sounds like my next stop. Where'd you say this place was, old timer?"

"Just a couple of blocks down the street there, then turn left up the alley. You can't miss it."

"Hey, thanks. You've been a big help, really."

"Don't mention it. Sure you wouldn't like some juice?"

"Maybe later. Right now I'm in a hurry."

The old man shook his head at her retreating back.

"That's the trouble with folks today. Everybody's in such a hurry. Don't you agree, big fella?"

Again I found myself torn between entering a conversation with this likable chap and watching over little sister. As always, family loyalty won out.

"Ahh . . . Big Crunch in hurry too. Will talk with little man later."

"Sure. Anytime. I'm usually around."

He waved goodbye, and I waved back as I hurried after Tananda.

Little sister seemed quite preoccupied when I caught up with her, so I deemed it wisest to keep silent as I fell in beside her. I assumed she was planning out her next move . . . at least, until she spoke.

"Tell me, big brother," she said, without looking at me. "What do you think of Bunny?"

Now Mums didn't raise any stupid children. Just Tananda and me. It didn't take any great mental gymnastics to figure out that perhaps this was not the best time to sing great praises of little sister's rival. Still, I would feel less than truthful, not to mention a little disloyal, if I gave false testimony when queried directly.

"Um . . . well, there's no denying she's attractive."

Tananda nodded her agreement.

". . . In a cheap, shallow sort of way, I suppose," she acknowledged.

"Of course," I said carefully, "she does have a little problem with overachievement."

"A *little* problem! Chumley, you have a positive talent for understatement. Bunny's one of the pushiest bitches I know."

I was suddenly quite glad I had not verbalized my thought comparing Bunny's overachievement problem with little sister's. I somehow doubted Tananda was in-

cluding herself in her inventory of pushy bitches. Still,
there was one more point I wanted to test the ice with.

"Then again, her performance may be influenced by
her infatuation with Skeeve."

At this, Tananda lashed out with her hand at a signpost
we were passing, which took on a noticeable tilt. Though
she isn't as strong as yours truly, little sister still packs
a wallop . . . especially when she's mad.

"That's the part that really grinds me," she snarled.
"If she thinks she can just waltz in out of left field and
take over Skeeve . . . I was about to say she'd have to
do it over my dead body, but it might give her ideas. I
don't really want to have tasters munching on my food
before I enjoy it. She's got another think coming, is all
I've got to say!"

I gave her my longest innocent stare.

"Why, little sister!" I said. "You sound positively
jealous. I had no idea you entertained any romantic designs on Skeeve yourself."

That slowed her pace a tad.

"Well, I don't, really. It's just that . . . blast it, Chumley, we helped raise Skeeve and make him what he is
today. You'd think he could do better than some primping
gold digger from Mobdom."

"And just what is he? Hmmm?"

Tananda shot me a look.

"I'm not sure I follow you there, big brother."

"Take a good look at what it is we've raised. Right
now Skeeve is one of the hottest, most successful magi-
cian/businessmen in the Bazaar. Who exactly do you
expect him to take up with for female companionship?
Massha? A scullery maid? Maybe one of the vendors or
come-on girls?"

"Well, no."

I had a full head of steam now. Tananda and I rarely talk seriously, and when we do it usually involves her dressing me down for some indiscretion or other. I wasn't about to let her slip away on this one.

"Of course Skeeve is going to start drawing attention from some pretty high-powered husband hunters. Whether we like it or not, the lad's growing up . . . and others are bound to notice, even if you haven't. In all honesty, little sister, if you met him today for the first time instead of having known him for years, wouldn't you find him a tempting morsel?"

"He's still a little young for me, but I see your point . . . and I don't tumble for just anybody."

"Since when?" I said, but I said it very quietly.

Tananda gave me a hard look, and for a moment I thought she had heard me.

"To hear you talk," she frowned, "I'd almost think you were in favor of a Bunny/Skeeve match-up."

"Her or somebody like her. Face it, little sister, the lad isn't likely to tie onto some nice, polite, 'girl-next-door' sort with his current life-style . . . and if he managed to, the rest of us would eat her alive in crackerjack time."

Tananda's pace slowed to almost a standstill.

"You mean that hanging around with us is ruining Skeeve's social life? Is that what you're trying to say?"

I wanted to take her by her shoulders and shake her, but even my gentlest shakes can be rather violent and I didn't want to get arrested for an attempted mugging. Instead, I settled for facing her with my sternest expression.

"Now, don't go all maudlin on me. What I'm trying to say is that Skeeve is used to associating with heavy hitters, so it's going to take a tougher-than-average lady fair to be comfortable around him, and vice versa. He'd be miserable with someone like that Luanna person.''

"What's wrong with Luanna?''

I shrugged and resumed our stroll, forcing Tananda to keep up.

"Oh, she's pretty enough, I suppose. But she's a small-time swindler who's so shortsighted she'd sell him out at the first hint of trouble. In short, she'd be an anchor around his neck who would keep him from climbing and potentially drag him down. If we're going to fix the lad up with a swindler, she should at least be a big-league swindler . . . like, say, a certain someone we know who has the Mob for a dowry.''

That at least got a laugh out of Tananda, and I knew we had weathered the storm.

"Chumley, you're incredible! And I thought women were manipulative matchmakers. I never realized it before, but you're a bit of a snob, big brother.''

"Think yew,'' I said in my best clipped accent. "I accept that observation with pride . . . when I consider the alternatives. I feel everyone would prefer to be snobs if they ever really had the choice.''

"Why are we stopping?''

"Well, if we're done deciding Master Skeeve's future for the moment, I believe we have a spot of business to attend to.''

She looked where I was pointing and found we were indeed standing in front of a dubious-looking establishment, embellished with a faded sign which proclaimed it to be the Suspended Sentence. The windows that weren't painted over were broken or gone completely, revealing a darkened interior. It might have been an abandoned building if it weren't for the definite sounds of conversation and laughter issuing forth from within.

Tananda started forward, then halted in her tracks.

"Wait a minute, big brother. What did you mean, 'we'?"

"Well, I thought that since I was here, I'd just . . ."

"Wrong," she said firmly. "This is still my assignment, Chumley, and I'm quite capable of handling it by myself."

"Oh, I wouldn't breathe a word."

"No, you'd just loom over everybody with that snaggletoothed grin of yours and intimidate them into cooperating with me. Well, you can just wait out here while I go in alone. I'll do my own intimidating, if you don't mind."

This was exactly the sort of thing I was afraid of.

"It would be less brutal if I were along," I argued weakly.

"Why, big brother," she said with a wink. "A little brutality never bothered me. I thought you knew that."

Outflanked and outmaneuvered, I had no choice but to lean against the wall and watch as she marched into the tavern.

"Oh, I know, little sister," I sighed. "Believe me, I know."

Though forbidden to take active part in the proceedings, I was understandably curious and kept one ear cocked to try to ascertain what was happening from the sound effects. I didn't have long to wait.

The undercurrent of conversation we had noted earlier ceased abruptly as Tananda made her entrance. A pregnant pause followed, then there was a murmured comment prompting a sharp bark of laughter.

I closed my eyes.

What happened next was so preordained as to be choreographed. I recognized little sister's voice raised in query, answered by another laugh. Then came the unmistakable sound of furniture breaking. No, that's not quite right. Actually, the noise indicated the furniture was being smashed, as in swung quickly and forcefully until an immovable object was encountered . . . like a head, for example.

The outcries were louder now, ranging from indignation to anger, punctuated by breaking glass and other such cacophonies. Years of hanging around with Tananda had trained my ear, so I amused myself by trying to catalogue the damage by its sound.

That was a table going over. . .

. . . Another chair . . . .

. . . A mirror (wonder how she missed the glasses?) . . . .

. . . That was definitely a bone breaking . . . .

. . . Someone's head hitting the bar, the side, I think . . . .

. . . *There* go the glasses . . . .

A body hurtled through the plate-glass window next to me and bounced once on the sidewalk before coming to a halt in a limp heap . . . a fairly good-sized one, too.

Unless I was mistaken, little sister was resorting to magic in this brawl or else she wouldn't have gotten that extra bounce on a horizontal throw. Either that or she was *really* annoyed! I debated whether or not to chide her for breaking our unwritten rules regarding no magic in barroom brawls, but decided to let it slide. On the off chance that she was simply overly perturbed, such comment would only invite retaliation, and Tananda can be quite a handful even when she isn't steaming.

By this time, the din inside had ceased and an ominous stillness prevailed. I figured it was jolly well time I checked things out, so I edged my way along the wall and peeked through the door.

With the exception of one lonely chair which seemed to have escaped unscathed, the place was a wreck with everything in splinters or tatters. Bodies, limp or moaning, were strewn casually about the wreckage, giving the overall effect of a battlefield after a hard fight . . . which, of course, it was.

The only surprising element in the scene was Tananda. Instead of proudly surveying the carnage, as was her normal habit, she was leaning against the bar chatting quietly with the bartender. This puzzle was rapidly solved, as the individual in question glanced up and saw my rather distinctive features in the doorway.

"Hey, Chumley! Come join us in a drink to my long-overdue remodeling."

Tananda glanced my way sharply, then nodded her approval.

"Come on in, big brother. You'll never guess who owns this dive."

"I think I just figured it out, actually," I said, helping myself to a drink from a broken bottle that was perched on the bar. "Hello, Weasel. Bit of a ways from your normal prowl grounds, aren't you?"

"Not anymore," he shrugged. "This is home sweet home these days. Can't think of anyplace else I've been that would let me operate as a respectable businessman."

Tananda gagged slightly on her drink.

"A respectable businessman? C'mon, Weasel. This is Tananda and Chumley you're talking to. How long have we known you? I don't believe you've had an honest thought that whole time."

Weasel shook his head sadly.

"Look around you, sweetheart. This is my place . . . or at least it used to be. Been running it fair and square for some time now. It may not be as exciting as my old lifestyle, but it's easily as profitable since I never lose any time in the slammer.''

Little sister was opening her mouth to make another snide remark when I elbowed her in the ribs. While I'm not above a bit of larceny myself from time to time, I figured that if Weasel genuinely wanted to go straight, the least we could do is not give him a hard time about it.

"So tell me, old chap," I said. "What brought about this amazing reform? A good woman or a bad caper?"

"Neither, actually. The way it was, see, was that I was framed . . . no, really, this time. I hadn't done a thing, but all the evidence had me pegged for being guilty as sin. I thought I had really had it, but this guy pops up and backs me hard. I mean, he springs for a really good mouthpiece, and when the jury finds me guilty anyway, he talks to the judge and gets me a suspended sentence. As if that weren't enough, after I'm loose again, he spots me the cash I need to start this place . . . a nice no-interest loan. 'Pay it back when you can,' he sez. I'll tell you, I ain't never had anybody believe in me like that before. Kinda made me think things over about how I was always saying that I had to be a crook 'cause no one would give me a fair shake. Well, sir, I decided to give the honest life a try . . . and haven't regretted it yet.''

"This mysterious benefactor you mentioned . . . his name wouldn't happen to be Hoos, would it?"

"That's right, Chumley. Easily the finest man I've ever met. You see, I'm not the only one he's helped out. Most of the people in this dimension have had some kind of hand up from him at one time or another. I'm not surprised you've heard of him.''

Tananda trotted out her best smile.

"That brings us to why I'm here, Weasel. I'm trying

to find this Hoos character, and so far the locals haven't been very helpful. Can you give me an introduction, or at least point me in a direction?''

The smile that had been on Weasel's face disappeared as if he had just been told he was left out of a rich uncle's will. His eyes lost their focus, and he licked his lips nervously.

"Sorry, Tananda," he said. "Can't help you there."

"Wait a minute, old buddy." Tananda's smile was a little forced now. "You must know where to find him. Where do you make your payments on this place?"

"Made the last payment half a year ago. Now if you'll excuse me . . ."

Tananda had him by the sleeve before he could take a step.

"You're holding out on me, Weasel," she snarled, abandoning any attempt at sweetness. "Now either you tell me where I can find this Hoos character or I'll . . ."

"You'll what? Wreck the place? You're a little late there, sweetheart. You want the last chair, be my guest. It doesn't match the rest of the decor now, anyway."

From little sister's expression, I was pretty sure what she was thinking of destroying wasn't the chair, so I thought I'd better get my oar in before things got completely out of hand.

"If you don't mind my asking, old chap, is there any particular reason you're being so obstinate over a simple request?"

Tananda gave me one of her "stay out of this" looks, but Weasel didn't seem to mind the interruption.

"Are you kidding?" he said. "Maybe you weren't listening, but I owe this guy . . . a lot more than just paying back a loan. He gave me a chance to start over

when everybody else had written me off. I'm supposed
to show my appreciation by setting a couple of goons on
his trail?''

''Goons?''

She said it very softly, but I don't think anyone in the
room mistook Tananda's meaning. In fact, a few of her
earlier playmates who were still conscious started crawl-
ing toward the door in an effort to put more distance
between themselves and the pending explosion.

Weasel, however, remained uncowed.

''Yeah, goons. What happened in here a few minutes
ago? An ice-cream social?''

''He's got you there, little sister.''

That brought her head around with a snap.

''Shut up, Chumley!'' she snarled. ''This is my assignment. Remember?''

''Wouldn't have it any other way. I do think Weasel
has a point, though. You really don't give the impression
of someone who wants a peaceful chat.''

At first I thought she was going to go for my throat.
Then she took a deep breath and blew it out slowly.

''Point taken,'' she said, releasing her grip. ''Weasel,
I really just want to talk to this guy Hoos. No rough
stuff, I promise.''

The bartender pursed his lips.

''I don't know, Tananda. I'd like to believe you. I
suppose if Chumley says it's on the up-and-up . . .''

That did it. Tananda spun on her heel and headed for
the door.

''If it takes Chumley's say-so, then forget it. Okay?
I'll do this my way, without help, even if it kills someone.''

''Hey, don't go away mad,'' Weasel called after her.
''Tell you what I'll do. When the police ask what hap-

pened here, I'll keep your name out of it, okay? I'll just play dumb and collect from the insurance. It'll kill my rates, but . . .''

"Don't ruin your new record on my account. Total up the damages and I'll cover the cost personally."

With that she slammed out into the street, cutting off any further conversation.

"Is she kidding?" Weasel said. "It's gonna cost a bundle to fix this place up again."

"I really don't know, old boy. She's really mad, but by the same token, she's mad enough that I wouldn't cross her. If I were you, I'd start totaling up the damages. Eh, what?"

"I hear that," he nodded. "Well, you'd better get after her before she gets into trouble. Sorry to be such a hard case, but . . .''

"Tut, tut," I waved. "You've been more than generous, all things considered. Well, cheerio."

I had expected to have to repeat my earlier performance of catching up with little sister, but instead I found her sitting on the curb just outside the bar. Now, she's not one to cry, either from anger or frustration, but seeing her there with her shoulders hunched and her chin in her hands, I realized that this might be one of those rare times.

"I say, you're really taking this quite hard, aren't you?" I said, as gently as I could.

She didn't look around.

"It's just that . . . oh, pook! Weasel's right, and so are you. I've been charging around like a bull in a china shop, and all that's been accomplished is that even my friends won't help me out. Bunny'll never let me forget it if I can't even pull off a simple collection assignment.''

Squatting beside her, I put a reassuring arm around her shoulders.

"I think that may be your problem, little sister. You're trying so hard to set a speed record to impress Bunny that you're rushing things . . . even for you. Now, I suggest that we retire someplace and think things through a bit, hmmm? Forget about getting the job done fast and just concentrate on getting it done."

That perked her up a bit, and she even managed a weak smile.

"Okay," she said. "Even though I still want to handle this on my own, I suppose there's nothing wrong with using you for a consultant since you're here. What I really feel like right now is a stiff drink to settle me down. I don't suppose you've spotted anyplace besides the Suspended Sentence where we could . . ."

"Care for a glass of juice?"

We looked up to find the old boy with his vending cart smiling down on us. For a moment I was afraid that Tananda would snap at him, but she gave him a grin that was far more sincere than her earlier smile.

"Thanks, but I had something stronger in mind. And while we're on the subject of thanks, I appreciate the information you gave me earlier . . . the second time, that is. I guess I was in too much of a hurry before to remember my manners."

"Don't mention it. It seems like most folks are in a hurry these days. Me, I always felt you should take your time and enjoy things. We've all got so little time, the least we should do is savor what time we have."

Tananda smiled at him with genuine warmth instead of her usual manipulative heat.

"That's good advice," she said. "I'll try to remember it. Come on, Chumley. We've got some planning to do . . . slow and careful planning, that is."

"Well, just holler if I can be of any help."

"Thanks, but what we really need is someone who can put us in touch with Mr. Hoos. I don't suppose you'd happen to know where I could find him?"

"Oh, that's easy."

"It is?"

I think we said it simultaneously. It was that kind of a surprise.

"Sure. Just stand up, blink three times, and he'll be right here."

That sounded a bit balmy to me, and for the first time I started doubting the old boy's sanity. Little sister, however, seemed to take him seriously. She was on her feet in the blink of an eye, blinking furiously.

"Well?" she said, peering around.

"Pleased to meet you, Missy. My name's Hoos. What's yours?"

We gaped at him . . . it seemed to be the logical thing to do at the time.

"You!?" Tananda managed at last. "Why didn't you say something before?"

"Didn't know until now it was me you were looking for."

It was really none of my business, but I had to ask.

"Just out of curiosity, why was it necessary for little sister to blink three times?"

As I spoke, I realized I had forgotten to use my Big Crunch speech patterns. Hoos didn't seem to notice:

"Wasn't, really. It's just you've been working so hard to find me, I thought I should throw in a little something to keep the meeting from being too anti-climactic. So, what can I do for you?"

There was a gleam of mischievousness in the old boy's

eye that led me to believe he wasn't as daft as he would like people to believe. Tananda missed it, though, as she fumbled a battered sheet of paper out of her tunic.

"Mr. Hoos," she said briskly. "I'm here representing a client who claims you owe him money on this old account. I was wondering when he could expect payment, or if you would like to set up a schedule for regular submissions?"

Hoos took the paper from her and studied it casually.

"Well, I'll be . . . I could have sworn I wrote him a check on this the next day."

"He did say something about a check being returned," Tananda conceded.

"Must of held onto it until I closed out. Darn! I thought I had covered everything."

"You closed out the account with the bank?"

Hoos winked at her.

"No, I closed out the bank. That was back when I was consolidating my holdings."

"Oh. Well, as I was saying, if you'd like to set up a payment schedule . . ."

He waved a hand at her and opened the top of his vending cart. From my height advantage, I could see that the bottom of it was filled with gold coins.

"Why don't we just settle up now?" he said. "I've got a little cold cash with me . . . get it? Cold cash? Let's see, you'll be wanting some interest on that . . ."

"MR. HOOS!"

We turned to find the bank manager striding rapidly toward us.

"I thought we agreed that you'd handle all your transactions through the bank! Carrying cash is an open invitation to the criminal element, remember?"

"What kind of a shakedown is going on here?" Weasel demanded, emerging from the door behind us. "This sure doesn't look like a friendly chat to me!"

A crowd was starting to form around us as people on the street drifted over and shopkeepers emerged from their stores. None of them looked particularly happy . . . or friendly.

"I know you want to handle this yourself, little sister," I murmured. "Would you mind if I at least showed my fangs to back some of this rabble off a ways? I want to get out of here alive, too."

"NOW JUST HOLD ON, *EVERYBODY*!"

Hoos was standing on the seat of his vending cart holding up restraining hands to the mob.

"This little lady has a legitimate bill she's collecting for. That's all. Now just ease off and go back to whatever you were doing. Can't a man do a little business in private any more?"

That seemed to placate most of the onlookers, and they began to disperse slowly. Weasel and the bank manager didn't budge.

"Let me see that bill," the manager demanded. "Do you recall incurring this debt, Mr. Hoos?"

"Yes, I recall incurring this debt, Mr. Hoos," Hoos said, mimicking the manager's voice. "Now, if you don't mind, I'll just pay it and the matter will be settled."

"Well, this is most irregular. I don't know why they didn't simply follow regular channels and present their claim at the bank."

"We *did* stop by the bank," Tananda snapped. "All we got was a runaround."

The manager peered at her.

"Oh, yes. I remember," he drawled. "What I don't

recall is your saying anything about submitting a claim for payment. There was some mention made of a bank robbery, though. Wasn't there?''

"You *were* moving a bit fast there, little sister," I chided gently.

"You mean to say you were working legit, Tananda?" Weasel chimed in. "Why didn't you say so in the first place?"

"I did! What's going on here, anyway, Weasel?"

"Mr. Hoos is a very rich man," the bank manager said. "He is also quite generous . . . sometimes too generous for his own good."

"It's my money, ain't it?" Hoos retorted. "Now, where were we? Oh, yes."

He started shoveling handfuls of coins into a paper bag.

". . . We were talking about interest on this bill. What do you think would cover the trouble I've caused missing payment the way I did?"

"See what we mean?" Weasel said. "Mr. Hoos, any interest due should have been set at the time of the debt. Paying any more would be just giving your money away."

The bank manager gave us a weak excuse for an understanding smile.

"As you can see, many of us in this dimension who owe our good fortune to Mr. Hoos have taken it upon ourselves to protect him from unnecessary expense . . . not to mention from those who would seek to take advantage of his generosity."

". . . After you've benefited from that generosity yourself," I added innocently.

That got a cackle of laughter out of Hoos.

"That's right, Big Fella," he said. "Don't think too

harshly of the boys, though. There's nothing quite as honest as a reformed criminal. Would you like me to tell you what the manager here was doing before I bailed him out?''

''I'd rather you didn't,'' the manager huffed, but there was a pleading note in his voice.

I saw that mischievous glint in the old boy's eyes again and found myself wondering for the first time who had *really* framed Weasel just before he decided to reform. I think little sister caught it too.

''I don't think any interest will be necessary, Mr. Hoos,'' she said, taking the bag from him. ''I'm sure my client will be happy with the payment as is.''

''Are you sure? Can't I give you a little something for your trouble?''

''Sorry. Company policy doesn't allow its agents to take tips. Weasel, you'll send me a bill for the damages to your place?''

''You got it, sweetheart,'' the bartender waved.

''There, now,'' Hoos said, reaching into his cart. ''I can cover that expense for you, at least.''

Tananda shook her head.

''It's baked into our operating budget. Really, Mr. Hoos, I'm already working legit. I really don't need any extra boosts. C'mon, Chumley. It's time we were going.''

Waving goodbye to the others, I took my place beside her as she started the gyrations to blip us through to our home base on Deva.

''Perhaps I shouldn't mention it, little sister,'' I said softly, ''but unless my eye for damage has deserted me completely, isn't that bill going to come to more than our company's share of the collection?''

"I said I'd cover it personally, and I will," she murmured back. "The important thing is that I've completed
this assignment in record time . . . and if you say anything
to Bunny about the damages, I'll make you wish you
had never been born. Do we understand each other, big
brother?"

Chapter Three:

"It's all a matter of taste."
—B. MIDLER

I REALLY HAVE to compliment you, dear. It never ceases to amaze me how much you do with so little."

That was Bunny's comment following Tananda's report on her last assignment. I had asked her to sit in to take notes, and I had to admit she had been extremely attentive while Tananda was speaking . . . which was more than I managed to do. From the report, the assignment was so routine as to be dull, though I personally wanted to hear Chumley's side of it before I made any final judgments on that score. That particular troll, however, was nowhere to be found . . . a fact which made me more than a little suspicious. Bunny was as efficient as ever, though, covering for my wandering thoughts by providing compliments of her own.

"Why, thank you, Bunny," Tananda purred back. "It really means a lot to me to hear you say that, realizing how much you know about operating with minimal resources."

It occurred to me that it was nice that these two were getting along as well as they did. Our operation could be a real mess if the two of them took to feuding.

It also occurred to me that there were an awful lot of teeth showing for what was supposed to be a friendly meeting. I deciaed it was time to move on to other subjects before things got *too* friendly.

"Things have been pretty quiet around here while you've been gone, Tananda," I said. "Not much new at all. How about it, Bunny? Any new prospects we should know about?"

Bunny made a big show of consulting her note pad. Right away, this alerted me. You see, I know that Bunny keeps flawless notes in her head, and the only time she consults her pad is when she's stalling for time trying to decide whether or not to bring something to my attention. I may be slow, but I *do* learn.

"Welll . . ." she said slowly. "The only thing I show at all is an appointment with somebody named Hysterium."

"Hysterium? Why does that name sound familiar? Wait a minute. Didn't I see a letter from him about a week back?"

"That's right. He's a land speculator and developer who's been trying to get in to see you for some time now."

"That shouldn't be a problem. What time is the appointment for?"

Bunny was staring at her notes again.

"Actually, I was thinking of postponing the meeting, if not canceling it altogether," she said.

"Why would we want to do that?"

I was annoyed, but curious. I really wasn't wild about Bunny trying to make my decisions for me. Still, she had a good head for business, and if this guy made her hesitate, I wanted to know why.

"It's like I was trying to tell you before, Skeeve. Your time is valuable. You can't just give it away to any fruitcake who wants an appointment."

". . . And you figure this guy's a fruitcake?"

"He must be," she shrugged. "What he wants to talk about simply isn't our kind of work. As near as I've been able to make out, he wants us to serve as interior decorators."

That brought Tananda into the conversation.

"You're kidding. Interior decorators?"

Bunny actually giggled and turned to Tananda conspiratorially.

"That's right. It seems he started building a motel complex counting on the fact that his would be the only lodging available in the area. Since he's started construction, though, four others have either announced their intentions to build or have started construction themselves . . right on his doorstep. Of course, since his original plan didn't include any competition, the design is more utilitarian than decorative. It's going to make his place look real shabby by comparison, and he's afraid of losing his shirt."

"That's bad," Tananda winced. "So what does he want us to do about it?"

"Well, apparently our outfit is getting a bit of a rep for being miracle workers . . . you know, 'If you're really up against a wall, call THEM!'? Anyway, he wants us to come up with an alternate design or a gimmick or something to catch people's attention so that his place will fill up before the competition rents out room one."

"Us? The man must be crazy."

"Crazy or desperate," Bunny nodded. "I know we'd

have to be crazy to take the job.''

I waited until they were done laughing before I ventured my opinion.

"I think we should take it,'' I said at last.

I suddenly had their undivided attention.

"Really? Why should we do that?''

I steepled my fingers and tried to look wise.

"First off, there's the fee . . . which, if I remember the letter correctly, was substantial even by our standards. Then again, there's the very point you were raising: we've never done anything like this before. It'll give us a chance to try something new . . . diversify instead of staying in a rut doing the same types of jobs over and over again. Finally . . .''

I gave them both a lazy smile.

". . . As you said, it's an impossible job, so we won't guarantee results. That means if we fail, it's what's expected, but if we succeed, we're heroes. The beauty of it is that either way we collect our fee.''

The women exchanged quick glances, and for a moment I thought they were going to suggest that I take an extended vacation . . . like, say, at a rest home.

"Actually,'' Bunny said slowly, "I did have a course in interior decorating once in college. I suppose I could give it a shot. It might be fun designing a place on someone else's money.''

"But, dear,'' Tananda put in, "you're so valuable here at the office. Since there's no guaranteed success on this one, it might be better if I took it on and left you free for more important assignments.''

Bunny started to say something in return, then glanced at me and seemed to change her mind.

"I suppose if your heart's set on it, there's no reason we couldn't *both* work on it together. Right, Skeeve?''

Now *that* had to be the dumbest idea I had heard all day. Even if the two of them were getting along fine now, I was sure that if they started butting heads over design ideas, any hope of friendship would go right out the window.

Fortunately, I had a solution.

"Sorry," I said carefully, "I actually hadn't planned on using either one of you on this assignment."

That hung in the air for a few moments. Then Tananda cleared her throat.

"If you don't mind my asking, if you aren't going to use either of us, who are you giving the assignment to?"

I came around my desk and perched on the edge so I could speak more personally.

"The way I see it, the new design will have to be attention-getting, a real showstopper. Now when it comes to eye-catching displays, I think we've got just the person on our staff."

Massha's Tale

"ARE YOU *SURE* the great Skeeve sent you?"

Now I'll tell ya, folks, I'm used to people overreactin' to me, but this guy Hysterium seemed to be gettin' a little out a hand. I mean, Deveels are supposed to be used to dealin' with all sorts of folks without battin' an eye. Still, he was the client, and business is business.

"What ya sees is what ya gets, Cute, Rich, and Desperate."

It never hurts to spread a little sugar around, but this time the customer just wasn't buyin'.

"*The* Great Skeeve? The one who runs M.Y.T.H. Inc.?"

This was startin' ta get redundant, so I decided it was

time ta put a stop to it once and for all. I heaved a big
sigh . . . which, I'll tell you, on me is really something.

"Tell ya what . . . Hysterium, is it? Never was much
good with *names*. If you want I'll go back and tell the
Prez that you decided not to avail yourself of our services.
Hmmm?"

All of a sudden, he got a lot more appreciative of what
he was gettin'.

"No! I mean, that won't be necessary. You . . . weren't
quite what I was expecting, is all. So you're agents of
M.Y.T.H. Inc., eh? What did you say your names were
again?"

I don't know what he was expecting, but I was willin'
ta believe we weren't it . . . at least, I wasn't. Even
when I'm just lazin' around I can be quite an eyeful, and
today I decked myself out to the nines just ta be sure to
make an impression. Of course, in my case it's more
like out to the nineties.

No one has ever called me petite . . . not even when
I was born. In fact, the nurses took ta calling my mom
the "Oooh-Ahh Bird," even though I didn't get the joke
until I was older. The fact of the matter is, folks, that
I'm larger than large . . . somewhere between huge and
"Oh, my God," leaning just a teensy bit toward the
latter. Now I figure when you're my size there's no way
to hide it, so you might as well flaunt it . . . and, believe
me, I've become an expert on flauntin' it.

Take for example my chosen attire for the day. Now
a lot of girls moan that unless you got a perfect figure,
you can't wear a bare midriff outfit. Well, I've proven
over and over again that that just isn't so, and today was
no exception. The top was a bright lime green with purple
piping, which was a nice contrast to the orange-and-red-
striped bottoms. While I feel there's nothing wrong with

going barefoot, I found these darling turquoise harem slippers and couldn't resist addin' them to the ensemble. Of course, with that much color on the bod, a girl can't neglect her makeup. I was usin' violet lipstick accented by mauve eye shadow and screaming yellow nail polish, with just a touch of rouge to hide the fact that I'm not gettin' any younger. I'd thought of dyein' my hair electric blue instead of its normal orange, but decided I'd stick with the natural look.

Now, some folks ask where I find outfits like that. Well, if ya can keep a secret, I have a lot of 'em made especially for me. Face it, ya don't find clothes like these on the rack . . . or if ya do, they never fit right. Be sure ta keep that a secret, though. The designers I patronize *insist* that no one ever find out . . . probably afraid they'll get swamped with orders. They never put their labels in my clothes for the same reason. Even though I've promised not to breathe a word to anybody, they're afraid someone might find out by accident . . . or was that *in* an accident? Whatever.

Oh, yes. I was also wearin' more than my normal allocation of jewelry, which, for anyone who knows me, means quite a lot. Ta save time, I won't try to list the whole inventory here. Just realize I was wearin' multiples of everything: necklaces, dangle bracelets, ankle bangles, earrings, nose rings . . . I went especially heavy on rings, seein' as how this was for work. You see, not only are my rings a substantial part of my magical arsenal, Mom always said it wasn't ladylike to wear brass knuckles, and my rings give me the same edge in a fight, with style thrown in for good measure.

Anyway, I really didn't blame the client for bein' a little overwhelmed when we walked in. Even though he bounced back pretty well, all things considered, I think

it took the two of us ta prove ta him just how desperate
he really was.

"Well, I'm Massha," I said, "and my partner over
there is Vic."

Hysterium nearly fell over his desk in his eagerness
to shake Vic's hand. My partner was dressed stylishly,
if sedately by my standards, in a leisure suit with a
turtleneck and ankle-high boots. His whole outfit was in
soft earth tones, and it was clear the Deveel had him
pegged as the normal member of the twosome. Call it a
mischievous streak, but I just couldn't let it stand at that.

"Actually, Vic isn't one of our regular staff. He's a
free-lancer we bring in occasionally as a specialist."

"A specialist?" Hysterium noted, still shakin' Vic's
hand. "Are you an interior decorator?"

My partner gave him a tight smile.

"No, I'm more of a night-life specialist. That's why
I'm wearing these sunglasses. I'm very sensitive to the
light."

"Night life? I'm not sure I understand."

I hid a little smile and looked at the ceiling.

"What Vic here is tryin' to say," I told the Deveel,
as casually as I could, "is that he's a vampire."

Hysterium let go of the hand he had been pumpin' like
it had bitten him.

"A vampire?!"

Vic smiled at him again, this time lettin' his outsized
canines show.

"That's right. Why? Have you got something against
vampires?"

The client started edgin' away across the office.

"No! It's just that I never . . . No. It's fine by me.
Really."

"Well, now that that's settled," I said, takin' command

of the situation again, "let's get down to business. If I understand it right, you've got a white elephant on your hands here and we're supposed to turn it into a gold mine by the first of the month."

Hysterium was gingerly seatin' himself behind his desk again.

"I . . . Yes. I guess you could summarize the situation that way. We're scheduled to be ready to open in three weeks."

". . . And what kind of budget have we got to pull this miracle off with?" Vic said, abandoning his "looming vampire" bit to lean casually against the wall.

"Budget?"

"You know, Big Plunger. As in 'money'?" I urged. "We know what our fees are. How much are you willin' to sink into decorations and advertisin' to launch this place properly?"

"Oh, that. I think I've got the figures here someplace. Of course, I'll be working with you on this."

He started rummagin' through the papers on his desk.

"Wrong again, High Roller," I said firmly. "You're going to turn everything over to us and take a three-week vacation."

The Deveel's rummagin' became a nervous fidget. I was startin' ta see how he got his name.

"But . . . I thought I'd be overseeing things. It *is* my project, after all."

"You thought wrong, Mister," Vic said. "For the next three weeks it's *our* project."

"Don't you want my input and ideas?"

Fortunately, Vic and I had talked this out on the way over, so I knew just what to say.

"Let me put it to you this way, Hysterium," I said. "If you had any ideas you thought would work, you'd be tryin' them yourself instead of hirin' us. Now, three weeks isn't a heck of a lot of time, and we can't waste any of it arguin' with you over every little point. The only way to be sure you don't yield to the temptation of kibitzin' and stay out from underfoot is for you not ta be here. Understand? Now make up your mind. Either you let us do the job without interference, or you do it yourself and we call it quits right now.''

The Deveel deflated slightly. It's always a pleasure doin' business with desperate people.

''Don't you at least need me to sign the checks?'' he asked weakly.

''Not if you contact the bank and tell 'em we're cleared to handle the funds,'' I smiled.

''While you're at it,'' Vic suggested, ''let the contractor know we'll be making a few changes in the finishing work his crew will be doing. Say that we'll meet him here first thing in the morning to go over the changes. Of course, we'll need to see the blueprints right away.''

Hysterium straightened up a little at that, glancin' quickly from one of us to the other.

''Can you at least let me in on your plans? It sounds like you have something specific in mind.''

''Not really, Sugar,'' I winked. ''We're just clearin' the decks so we can work. The marchin' orders are to turn a third-rate overnight hotel into the biggest tourist trap Deva has ever seen. Now will you get movin' so we can get started?''

It took us quite a while to go over the blueprints. You see, buildin' things had never been a big interest of mine, so it took a while to understand what all the lines and notes meant. Fortunately, Vic had studied a bit of architecture at one point when he was thinkin' of givin' up magic, so he could explain a lot of it to me . . . or at least enough so I could follow what he was talkin' about.

"Let's face it, Massha," he said at last, leanin' back in his chair. "No matter how long we stare at the drawings, they aren't going to change. What he's built here is a box full of rooms. The place has about as much personality as an actuary . . . which is to say, a little less than an accountant."

"You gotta admit, though," I observed, "the setup has a lot of space."

I could see why our client was nervous. The place was plain, but it was five floors of plain spread over a considerable hunk of land. There was a lot of extra land for expansion, which at the moment seemed unlikely. Hysterium had obviously sunk a bundle into puttin' this deal together, money he would never see again if nobody rented a room here.

"Tell me, Vic. Your home dimension is entertainment-oriented enough so that the competition for crowds has to be pretty heavy. What's packin' 'em in these days, anyway?"

The vampire frowned for a few moments as he thought over my question.

"Well, it depends on what kind of clientele you're after. You can go after the family groups or folks who have already retired. My favorite is the young professionals. They usually haven't started their families yet or are passing on them completely, which means they've got both money and time. For that set, clubs are always big. It I really wanted to pull crowds into a new place, I'd probably open a good disco."

"Now we're talkin'. Do you think you could put one together in three weeks?"

My partner shook his head and laughed.

"Hold on a second, Massha. I was just thinking out loud. Even if I could come up with a plan for a club, there's no room for it."

Now it was my turn ta laugh.

"Vic, honey, if there's one thing we've got it's room. Look here . . ."

I flipped the blueprints to the drawin's of the first floor.

". . . What if we knocked out the inside walls here on the ground level? That'd give us all the space we'd ever need for your disco."

"Too much space," the vampire said, studyin' the plans. "The key to one of these clubs is to keep it fairly small so people have to wait to get in. Besides, I'm afraid if we knocked out *all* the internal walls, there wouldn't be enough support for the rest of the structure."

An idea was startin' ta form in my head.

"So try this. We keep the whole outer perimeter of rooms . . . turn 'em into shops or somethin'. That'll give extra support and cut back on your club space. And if that's still too big . . ."

"About four times too big."

"Uh huh. What would you say ta a casino? I haven't seen one yet that didn't draw tourists by the droves."

Vic expressed his admiration with a low whistle.

"You don't think small, do you? I'm surprised you aren't thinking of a way to make money off the grounds as well."

"I can't make up my mind between a golf course and an amusement park," I said. "That can wait for a while until we see how the rest of this works out."

Right about then, I noticed Vic babes had his cheaters off and was studyin' me. Now, I'm used to bein' stared at, but there was somethin' kinda unsettlin' about his expression that was outside the norm, if ya know what I mean. I waited for him ta speak his mind, but after a while the silence started gettin' to me.

"What're you lookin' at me that way for, Young and Bloodthirsty? Did I grow another head sudden-like when I wasn't lookin'?"

Instead of answerin' right away, he just kept starin' until I was thinkin' a bustin' him one just ta break the suspense.

"You know, Massha," he said finally, "for a so-called apprentice, you're pretty savvy. With the way you dress and talk it's easy to overlook, but there's quite a mind lurking behind all that mascara, isn't there?"

Now if there's one thing I have trouble handlin' it's praise . . . maybe 'cause I don't hear that much of it. To keep my embarrassment from bein' too noticeable, I did what I always do and ducked behind a laugh.

"Don't let the wrappin' fool ya, Fangs. Remember, I used ta be an independent before I signed on with Skeeve's gang. Magician for the city-state of Ta-hoe and then Vey-gus over on Jahk, that was me."

"Really? I didn't know that."

Just goes to show how rattled I was. I couldn't even remember how little Vic knew about our operation and the people in it.

"That was when I first ran into the Boy Wonder. He was in trouble then, too . . . in fact, Skeeve seems to have a knack for trouble. Remind me sometime to tell you about the spot he was in when I *did* join up."

"Why not now?" he said, leanin' back in his chair. "I'm not going anywhere, and there's no time like the present for learning more about one's business associates."

As you've probably noticed, I was eager to get off the spot, and talkin' about Skeeve seemed to be just the ticket I was lookin' for.

"Well, at the time his big green mentor had taken off for Perv, see . . . some kinda family problem. Anyway, the king puts the touch on Skeeve to stand in for him, supposedly so's his royalness could take a bit of a vacation . . . say, for a day or so. What the Man neglected to mention to our colleague was that his bride-to-be, a certain Queen Hemlock, was due ta show up expectin' ta tie the knot with whoever was warmin' the throne just then."

"Queen Hemlock?"

"Let me tell you, she was a real sweetheart. Probably would have ended up on the gallows at an early age if she hadn't been the daughter of a king. As it was, she ended up runnin' the richest kingdom in that dimension and was out to merge with the best military force around . . . which turned out to be the kingdom that Skeeve was babysittin'."

Vic frowned.

"If she was already in a position to buy anything she wanted; what did she need an army for?"

"For those doodads that *weren't* for sale. You see, we all have our little dreams. Hers was to rule the world. That was Queen Hemlock for you. The morals of a mink in heat and the humble aspirations of Genghis Khan."

"And the two of you stopped her?"

"To be truthful with you, Skeeve did. All I did was round up the king so we could put him back on the throne where he was supposed to be. Skeeve set 'em up with a pair of wedding rings that never come off which also link their lives. That meant if Queenie wanted to off Kingie and clear the path for a little world-conquering, she'd be slitting her own throat at the same time."

"Where'd he find those? I never heard of such a thing."

I gave him a chuckle and a wink.

"Neither has anyone else. What they got was some junk jewelry from a street vendor here at the Bazaar along with a fancy story concocted by one Skeeve the Great. What I'm sayin' is that he sold 'em a line of hooey, but it was enough to cool Hemlock's jets. Smooth move, wasn't it?"

Instead of joinin' in with my laughter, the vampire thought for a few moments, then shook his head.

"I don't get it," he said. "Now, don't mistake me . . . I think Skeeve's a swell guy and all that. It's just that from all I can find out, he doesn't use all that much magik, and what he does use is pretty weak stuff. So how has he built up an organization of top-flight talent around him like you and the others?"

"I'll tell ya, Vic, there's magik and there's magik. Skeeve has . . . how can I explain it? He may not be strong in the bibbity-bobbity-boo department, and he hasn't got the woman sense of a Quasimodo, but he's got enough heart for three normal folks."

I punched him lightly on the arm.

"Remember when I said he has a knack for gettin' into trouble? Well, the truth is that more often than not he's bailin' someone else out who really deserves to get what's comin' to 'em. In that Hemlock caper I was just tellin' you about, he could have headed for the horizon once he figured out that he'd been had . . . but that would have left a whole kingdom without a leader, so he stuck it out. When I met him, he was workin' at gettin' Tananda loose after she got pinched tryin' ta steal a birthday present for Aahz. Heck, as I recall, the first time we crossed paths with you we were settin' up a jailbreak for his old mentor. That's Skeeve, if ya see what I mean. He's always gettin' in over his head tryin' ta do what he thinks is right, and a body gets the feelin' . . . I don't know, that if you stand beside him he just might be able to pull it off. Even if it don't work out, you feel you've been doin' somethin' good with your life instead of just hangin' in there for the old number one. Am I makin' any sense at all?''

"More than you know," Vic said. "If I'm understanding you properly, he sets a high personal standard, and consequently draws people to him who are impressed by the sincerity of his actions . . . who in turn try to match the proportionate output they perceive in him. It's an interesting theory. I'll have to think about it.''

I couldn't help but notice that once old Fangs got wrapped up in somethin', he started soundin' more like a college prof than a night-lovin' partygoer. It made me a little curious, but since I don't like people tryin' to peek at more of me than I'm willin' to show, I decided to let it go.

"Speakin' a theories," I said, "we got one that isn't goin' to work itself out without a lotta pushin' from us.''

The vampire stretched his arms and yawned.

"All right. I'll take care of the disco and the architect if you can start checking into the casino and the shops. Okay?''

I had to admit I was a little taken aback by his enthusiasm.

"You mean right now? It's pretty late.''

He showed me his fangs in a little grin.

"For you, maybe. Us night people are just starting to wake up, which means it's just the right time for me to start scouting around for a band and bar staff. Since we're on different missions anyway, though, I've got no problem if you want to catch a few Z's before you do your rounds. What say we meet here same time tomorrow for an update?''

Now, folks, I may strut a bit and loud-talk even more, but I'll also be the first to admit that little Massha doesn't know everythin'. One of the many things I know next ta nothin' about is how ta run a casino. Considerin' this, it was easy ta see I was goin' ta require the services of an expert . . . in casinos, that is.

It took me a while to locate him, but I finally ran my mark to ground. He was slouched at a back table in a dingy bar, and from the look of him things hadn't been goin' real good. I was glad ta see that . . . not that I wished him ill, mind you; it just made my sales pitch a little easier.

"Hiya, Geek," I said, easin' up to his table. "Mind if I join ya?"

He blinked his eyes a couple times tryin' ta focus 'em before he realized that the person talkin' to him really was that big.

"Well, well, well. If it isn't one of the M.Y.T.H. Inc. hotshots. What brings you to this neck of the woods, Massha? Slumming?"

I pulled up a chair so's I could sit close to him. I mean, he hadn't said no, and that's about as close to an invitation as I usually get.

"I know you're busy, Geek, so I'll give it to ya straight. We're cookin' up a little deal and I'd like you to be a part of it. Interested?"

"Well, whaddaya know. After making me sell my club and putting me out on the street, the Great Skeeve has a deal for me. Isn't that just ducky!"

Now I may not know casinos, but I know drunk when I see it. Seein' as how it was just sunset, which for the Geek is like early morning, he was in pretty bad shape. The trouble was, I needed him sober. Normally I'd a taken him off someplace and let him sleep it off, but I was in a hurry. This called for drastic action.

Glancin' around the place to be sure there were no witnesses, I leaned forward, wrapped my arms around his neck, and gave him the biggest, juiciest kiss I knew. One of the other things I know more than a little about is kissin', and this particular sample lasted a fairly long time. When I felt him startin' ta struggle for air, I let go and leaned back.

"Wha . . . Who . . . Massha!" he said, gaspin' like a fish out of water. "What happened?"

I batted my eyelashes at him.

"I don't think I catch your drift, Big Red."

The Geek just sat there blinkin' for a few seconds, one hand on the top of his head like he was afraid it was goin' ta come off.

"I . . . I don't know," he managed at last. "I've been drunk for . . . what day is it? Never mind! . . . for a long time. Now all of a sudden I'm wide awake and stone cold sober. What happened? How long have you been here?"

I smiled ta myself and mentally accepted a pat on the back. My record was still intact. I've been told more times than you can count that nothin' sobers a body up as completely or as fast as a little hug and a kiss from Massha.

"Just long enough to catch the curtain goin' up," I said. "Now that we're all present and accounted for, though, I want ya ta listen close to a little proposition."

The Geek used ta be one of the biggest bookies at the

Bazaar. At one point, he had his own club, called the Even Odds. Of course, that was before Skeeve caught him usin' marked cards and suggested strongly that he sell us his club. I wasn't sure how the Prez would react to my cuttin' the Geek in on this new project, but he was the only one I could think of who had the necessary knowledge to set up a casino and was currently unemployed.

"I don't know, Massha," he said after I had explained the situation. "I mean, it sounds good . . . but a casino's a big operation. I'm not exactly rolling in investment capital right now."

"So start small and build. Look, Geek, the house is going ta be providin' the space and decor rent free. All you have ta do is set up security and round up some dealers to work the tables."

"Did you say 'rent free'?"

It occurred ta me that maybe I shouldn't have sobered him up quite so much. Now he was back ta thinkin' like a Deveel bookie.

"Well . . . practically. The way I figure it, the house will take a piece of the action, which means you'll only have ta pay rent if you lose money."

"That's no problem," the Geek said with a smile. "With the dealers I'm thinking of, there's no way we'll end up in the red."

Somehow, I didn't like the sound of that.

"I hope it goes without sayin' that we expect you ta run a clean operation, Geek," I warned. "I don't think the Great Skeeve would like ta be part of settin' up a crooked casino. Content yourself with the normal winnings the odds throw the house. Okay?"

"Massha! You wound me! Have I ever run anything but a clean game?"

I gave him a hard stare, and he had the decency to flush slightly.

"Only once that I know of," I said, "and if I recall correctly it was Skeeve who caught you at it that time. If I were you, I'd keep my nose clean . . . unless you want ta wake up some morning on a scratchy lily pad."

The Geek sat up a little straighter and lost his smug grin.

"Can he really do that?"

"It was just a figure of speech, but I think you catch my meanin'. Just remember, the only times you've lost money on your crew is when you got suckered into bettin' against us."

"That's true," the Deveel said with a thoughtful nod. "Speaking of Skeeve, are you sure there won't be a problem there? The last time I saw him we weren't on the best of terms."

"You worry about the casino and leave Skeeve ta me," I smiled confidently, hopin' I knew what I was talkin' about. "Anyway, Skeeve's not one ta hold a grudge. If memory serves me correctly, Aahz was all set ta tear your throat out that last meeting, and it was Skeeve who came up with the suggestion that let you off the hook with your skin intact."

"True enough," the Geek nodded. "The Kid's got class."

"Right. Oh! Say, speakin' a class, you might try to run down the Sen-Sen Ante Kid and offer him a permanent table of his own."

The Deveel cocked his head at me.

"No problem, but do you mind my asking why?"

"Well, the last time he was in the vicinity for that match-up with Skeeve, I got stuck baby-sitting that character assassin you fobbed off on us. That means I'm the only one a our team who didn't get a chance ta meet him . . . and, from what I hear, he's my kinda guy. Besides, he might appreciate settlin' down instead of hoppin' from game to game all the time. Aren't any of us gettin' any younger, ya know."

"Ain't that the truth," the Geek said with a grimace. "Say, that might not be such a bad idea. Having the best Dragon Poker player at the Bazaar as a permanent player at the casino would be a pretty good draw."

We talked a while more, but it was all detail stuff. The Geek was on board, and the casino was startin' ta take shape.

Casinos may not be my forte, but nobody knows retail stores like yours truly. Bunny may be aces when it comes ta findin' class outfits at decent prices, and Tananda sure knows her weapons, but when it comes ta straight-at-ya, no-holds-barred shoppin', they both take a back seat ta Massha.

I had noticed this place long before the assignment came up, but it stuck in my mind so I thought I'd check it out. There were big "Going Out Of Business" and "Everything Must Go" sale signs all over the window, but they had been there for over a year, so I didn't pay 'em much heed.

For a storefront shop, the place was a disaster. Their stock could only be described as "stuff" . . . and that's bein' generous. There were T-shirts and ash trays and little dolls all mixed in with medications and magazines in no particular order. The shelves were crammed with a small selection of the cheap end of everything. They didn't have as many clothing items as a clothing store, as many hardware items as a hardware store . . . I could go on, but you get the point. If you wanted selection or quality in anything, you'd have ta go somewhere else. In short, it was just the sort of place I was lookin' for.

"Can I help you, lady?"

The proprietor was perched behind the counter on a stool readin' a newspaper. He didn't get up when he talked ta me, so I decided ta shake him up a little.

"Well, yes. I was thinkin' a buyin' a lot of . . . stuff. Can you give me some better prices if I buy in volume?"

That brought him out from behind the counter with a pad and pencil which had materialized out of thin air.

"Why, sure, lady. Always ready to deal. What was it you were thinking of?"

I took my time and looked around the place again.

"Actually, I was wonderin' if you could quote me a price on everything in the store."

"Everything? Did you say everything?"

"Everything . . . including your sweet adorable self."

"I don't understand, lady. Are you saying you want to buy my store?"

"Not the store, just what's in it. I'm thinkin' this place could do better in a new location. Truthfully now, how has business been going for you lately?"

The owner tossed his pad and pencil back onto the counter.

"Honestly? Not so hot. My main supplier for this junk just raised his prices . . . something about a new union in his factory. I either gotta raise my prices, which won't help, since this stuff is hard enough to move as it is, or go out of business, which I've seriously been considering."

I thought it would be best not to comment on the union he'd mentioned.

"You don't think a new location would help?"

"New location . . . big deal! This is the Bazaar at

Deva, lady. One row of shops is like any other for pedestrian traffic. On any one of those rows you can find better stuff than I got to sell.''

This was turnin' out ta be even better than I had hoped.

''Just suppose,'' I said, ''just suppose the new location was in a hotel, and suppose that hotel had a casino and disco. That would give you a captive clientele, since nobody wants ta leave the building and wander around to find somethin' they can buy right where they are.''

''A hotel and casino, eh? I dunno, though. Junk is still junk.''

''Not if you had an exclusive to print the name of the place on everythin' you sell. Junk with a name on it is souvenirs, and folks expect ta pay more for them. Right?''

The proprietor was startin' ta get excited.

''That's right! You got a place like this, lady? How much ya asking for rent?''

''Minimal, with a piece of the action goin' ta the house. How does that sound?''

''How much floor space do you have available? If I can expand, I can get a volume discount from my supplier and *still* raise my prices. Say, do you have a printer lined up yet?''

''Hadn't really thought about it.''

''Good. I got a brother-in-law who does good work cheap . . . fast, too. How about a restaurant? All those folks gotta eat.''

Now that was one that had slipped by both Vic and me.

''A restaurant?''

''. . .'Cause if you don't, I know a guy who's been looking to move his deli since they raised the rent on the place he's got.''

I had a feelin' my problems with the storefronts was solved.

"Tell ya what, Well Connected. You pass the word ta the folks you think would fit into this deal, and I'll be back tomorrow with the floor plans. We can fight out who gets which space then."

All in all, things went fairly smoothly carryin' out our plans for the revised hotel. It turned out, though, that for all our figurin' there was one detail we overlooked.

"We need a name!" Vic moaned for the hundredth time as he paced the office.

I looked up from where I was doodlin' on Hysterium's desk pad.

"What was he going to call it again?"

"The Hysterium Inn."

"Really, is it all that bad for a name?"

We looked at each other.

"Yes," we said at the same time.

"We could come up with a better name in our sleep."

"Terrific, Vic. What have you got?"

"Beg pardon?"

"The name. You said you could come up with a better one in your sleep."

"I said *we* could come up with a better name in our sleep. This is supposed to be a team, you know."

I shrugged helplessly.

"I'm not asleep."

"We need a name!" my teammate moaned for the hundred and first time.

"Look on the bright side, Fangs. At least we don't have ta overcome an established advertisin' campaign."

The vampire plopped into a chair.

"You can say that again," he growled. "I don't believe how cheap that Deveel is. He was going to open without any advertising at all!"

"Zero competition, remember? If you're figurin' on bein' the only game in town, you don't have ta advertise."

"Well, I think we can kiss the idea of bringing this job in under budget goodbye," Vic said grimly. "Sorry, Massha. I know how hard you've worked cutting corners expense-wise."

"Forget it," I waved. "How do you figure we should promote this place, anyway?"

"The usual newspaper ads aren't going to be enough . . . even though we'll have to do them anyway. This close to opening, we're going to have to come up with something extra to get the word out."

"How about billboards?"

Vic scrunched up his face.

"I don't know, Massha. I don't think a couple of billboards will do it."

"I was thinkin' more like lotsa billboards . . . more like fifty of them blanketin' the area for a ten-mile radius."

". . . Widely spaced further out, and closer together the nearer you get," he added thoughtfully. "I like it! Of course, it'll cost."

"So I shave a little here and there on the decorations. We'd better get on those right away. Nothin' too classy, mind you. We don't want to scare anybody away. What we need is someone who does the signs for the Reptile Farms. That kinda excitement."

"I know just the guy," Vic said, scribblin' down a note. "That brings us back to our original problem."

"Right. We need a name."

The vampire's head came up with a snap.

"Hey! That's my line."

"Sorry."

"This is the pits, you know?"

"How about that? The Pitts?"

"No. How about the Funny Farm?"

"Uh-uh. The Snake Pit?"

"Will you get off pits?"

"Well, then, how about . . ."

What we finally settled on was The Fun House. Our judgment was influenced a bit by the fact that I managed to locate a down-at-the-heels carnival. We let 'em set up on our grounds, and they gave us our pick of their displays for decorations.

The best of the lot was the outsized figures they had on top of their rides . . . and particularly The Fun House. These figures were of bein's from all over the dimensions and were animated to move their arms and heads while hidden speakers went "Ho Ho Ho" at passersby. I thought they were terrific and had them installed all over the outside of the hotel . . . except for the Fat Lady. Her I had installed in the men's john off the lobby.

Once we had that, the rest of the decorations fell into place. There wasn't much we could do to make the shape of the building excitin', so I had it painted with wide stripes . . . like a circus tent, only with more colors.

Vic did the disco, and it was a beaut. He did the whole place in black: floors, walls, ceiling, furniture, everything. He also attached chairs and tables to the walls and ceiling at different angles with life-sized dummies in evening attire. The overall effect was one of disorientation, so that when the band was goin' and the lights flashin', you weren't really sure which way was up. To add to the effect, the dance floor was slanted a bit and rotated slowly. It was like bein' suspended in space and bein' buffeted by cosmic winds and gravity at the same

time. He even named the club "The Pit" in appreciation
of me and to apologize for comin' down so hard on the
name when I suggested it for the hotel.

The casino was all mine, and I decided ta go for broke.
I found a painter with a sense of humor, and we did the
place in camouflage . . . except instead of usin' greens
and browns, we leaned heavy on the basic colors in
day-glo shades. For a crownin' touch, we spaced mirrors
all around the place, but we used the distortion mirrors
from the carnival Fun House. This not only gave the
place the illusion of bein' larger, but when the customers
glanced at themselves in the mirrors, they had the same
kind of meltin' lines as the decor. It definitely raised
questions in the mind as to exactly which reality we were
operatin' in.

Vic was afraid the impact of the whole operation was
a bit bright, but I argued that the whole idea was ta stand
out from the crowd and let people know we were there.
I did, however, unbend enough to agree that we should
have Skeeve on hand for our meetin' with Hysterium the
night before our opening. I mean, negotiatin' never was
my strong suit, and I had no idea how the client was
going to react to our rather innovative ideas.

"You've ruined me! That's what you've done! Ruined
me!"

That was our client speakin'. You may guess from the
sound of it that he was less than pleased with our work.
When you realize that that was how he was soundin'
after we had spent an hour calmin' him down, you've
got an idea of exactly how unhappy he was.

"I'm not sure I understand what your problem is, Mr.
Hysterium," Vic said. "If you have a complaint . . ."

"A complaint?" the Deveel shrieked. "I wouldn't

know where to start! What did you people think you were
doing, anyway?''

"We were turnin' your dump into a profit-makin'
hotel. That's what we were supposed to do.''

I was tryin' to stay out of this 'cause a my temper,
but I had to get a word or two in here somewhere.

"A hotel? A hotel? This isn't a hotel! What I left you
with was a hotel! What I came back to is a sideshow!
And what do *you* mean by profitable? All the rooms on
the first floor are gone! That cuts my rental earnings by
twenty percent!''

"Twenty percent of an empty hotel is still nothing!''
I shot back.

"Massha's right,'' Vic said, stepping between us.
"We needed that space for attractions to draw in some
customers. Besides, everything we put in there generates
revenues for the hotel.''

"Not if they don't sell anything!'' Hysterium argued.
"Have you been in any of those places? Have you seen
the junk they're selling? And the prices . . . they're
charging more for a cup of coffee in that club you put
in than I'm used to paying for a whole meal!''

"Not everybody eats as cheap as you do,'' I muttered
under my breath.

"What?''

"I said you stand ta clear a heap when they do . . .
sell stuff to the customers, that is.''

"But there aren't going to be any . . . Ohhh! I'm
ruined!''

The Deveel sank into a chair and hid his face in his
hands.

"Of course, if you had wanted design approval, you
should have stayed around. As it was, Massha and Vic
had no recourse but to use their own judgment.''

That was Skeeve speakin' from his chair in the corner.
So far, he hadn't done much more than listen to the
rantings.

"Stayed around?" Hysterium's head came up with a
snap. "They made me go! They said I'd have to trust
them if I wanted to use your outfit's services."

"Precisely," Skeeve nodded, changin' tactics without
batting an eye. "You wanted our services, you trusted
us, and we serviced you. I don't see what the complaint
is."

"What the complaint is, is that you charged me an
arm and a leg . . . in advance . . . to put me out of
business! If I had lost money on a regular hotel it would
have been bad enough, but to lose money *and* be made
a laughing-stock to boot . . . ." There were tears formin'
in the developer's eyes. "That was my wife's family
money I invested. I could turn a profit if I only had the
capital, I told them. Now . . ."

His voice broke and his head sank again.

"If that's the only problem, maybe we can work something out."

"Forget it! Cutting your fee wouldn't help. I need to
make money, not lose less."

"Actually, I was thinking more of taking the hotel off
your hands. Buying it outright."

I shot a glance at Skeeve. He was leanin' back in his
chair studyin' the ceiling.

"Are you serious?" the Deveel said hopefully.

"Why not? That way you turn a profit of . . . say,
fifteen percent over cost? . . . for the building and land,
and making the place work, much less dealing with its
reputation, will be our problem. That's what we agreed
to do in the first place . . . sort of."

Hysterium was on his feet pumpin' Skeeve's hand

almost before the Prez had stopped talkin'.

"I'll tell you, Skeeve . . . Mr. Skeeve . . . you're a real gent. This is terrific! Just when I thought . . . I can't tell you how much I appreciate . . ."

"Don't mention it," Skeeve said, retrievin' his hand. "Why don't you go on over to my office right now? My secretary is still there. Just explain everything to her, and she'll start drawing up the papers. I want to have a few words with my agents, then I'll be along to sign off on the deal."

"On my way," the Deveel waved. "Gee. I can't get over . . ."

"Now, you realize, of course, we don't have that kind of cash on hand. We'll have to give a down payment and arrange some kind of payment schedule."

"Fine. Fine. As long we get a contract guaranteeing my profit."

Then he was gone, leavin' us ta stare at each other in silence. Finally, Skeeve gathered us up with his eyes.

"The placed is booked solid?" he said, confirmin' what we had told him in our debriefing.

". . . For three weeks, with a waiting list for cancellations," Vic confirmed. "We're taking reservations for as much as a year and a half in advance."

". . . And Hysterium doesn't know?"

"He never asked, and we never got the chance to tell him," I shrugged. "You saw how he was."

Skeeve nodded thoughtfully.

"That means, if my calculations are correct, we'll be able to pay him off in full in less than three months . . . not including the take from the casino and the shops."

He rose and stretched, then gave us a wink.

"C'mon, you two," he said. "I think I'll invest an arm and a leg and buy you both a drink!"

Chapter Four:

"If you're too busy to help your friends, you're too busy!"

—L. IACOCCA

ACTUALLY, I WASN'T all that wild over The Fun House. I mean, it was making us money hand over fist, but I somehow never figured on owning a hotel/casino. In particular, I didn't think it was a good idea to set the precedent of buying out dissatisfied customers, no matter how profitable the deal turned out to be. As it was, Hysterium's relatives (on his wife's side) were trying to get the deal invalidated on the basis that he must have been out of his mind, or at least not in his right mind, to sell such a lucrative business at the price he did. I wasn't particularly worried, as this was still the Bazaar at Deva, and if everyone who signed off on a bad deal here was declared insane, the economy would collapse.

The part that really bothered me about the deal was that it meant associating with the Geek again. In past dealings with him, he had consistently proven to be primarily concerned with lining his own pockets without

much regard for anyone else, and I felt it was dangerous
to place him in a position where he had such temptingly
easy access to our money, or even a piece of it.

Still, I couldn't argue with Massha's logic in including
him in the scheme, and at the time she approached him
she had no idea he was going to end up reporting to us.
Bunny assured me that she was personally auditing the
financial reports for the casino that the Geek turned in
along with our share of the take, but I found that in spite
of that I tended to spend inordinate amounts of time
studying the spreadsheets myself, half expecting to find
some indication that he was somehow skimming a little
off the top for his personal accounts.

That's what I was doing this particular afternoon, setting aside the countless letters and chores that were pressing on my time to take one more pass at auditing the
Geek's financial reports. Bunny had told me once that a
hefty percentage of accountants and financial analysts
operated more out of spite than from any instinctive or
learned insight. That is, rather than detecting that there's
anything wrong from the figures they study, they single
out some department that's been giving them grief or a
manager who made snide comments about them at the
company party, then go over their reports *very* carefully.
She maintains that anyone's reports will come up flawed
or suspicious if reviewed closely enough.

That may well be, if one is a skilled numbers cruncher.
All I discovered was that prolonged periods of time spent
staring at rows of little numbers are a pain . . . literally
and figuratively. Specifically, after a few hours hunched
over the reports, I was feeling cramps and stabbing pain
in my eyes, my neck, my back, and regions lower.

Leaning back to ease the strain and stretching a bit,

my eye fell on the pencil I had tossed down on my desk from disgust and frustration. With a smirk, I reached out with my mind, grabbed it, and flipped it into the air. What do magicians do when they get bored or depressed? Tinker around with magik, natch!

Remember once upon a time when I used to sweat and groan to levitate a feather? Well, those days are long gone. Nothing like a few years of using the basics like levitation to save your skin to increase one's confidence . . . and, as Aahz always told me, confidence is the key to magik.

I took the pencil up to the ceiling, paused, then took it on a tour of the room, stopping cold at each corner to give it a right-angle turn. I realized I was humming a little tune under my breath as I put it through its paces, so I brought it down over the desk and started using it like a conductor's baton, cueing the drums and the horns as the tune built.

"Nice to see you're keeping your hand in."

I glanced over at the door, and discovered my old mentor leaning against the frame watching me work.

"Hi, Aahz," I said, keeping the pencil moving smoothly. "Well, things have been so busy I haven't had much time to practice, but I do still turn a spell now and then."

As offhand as I sounded, I was secretly very pleased that the pencil hadn't wavered when Aahz surprised me. Not breaking concentration on a spell, or, rather, maintaining a spell once concentration was broken, had been one of the harder lessons Aahz had taught me, and I thought I finally had it down pat. I only hoped he noticed.

"Got a few minutes for your old partner?"

"Sure, pull up a chair."

I decided it would be rude to keep playing with the pencil while I was talking to Aahz, so I brought it down to where I could pluck it smoothly from the air as I leaned forward. Aahz didn't seem to notice, though. He was craning his neck slightly to look at the papers scattered across my desk.

"What's all this?"

"Oh, just going over the financials from The Fun House. I still don't trust the Geek completely."

Aahz settled back in his chair and cocked his head at me.

"The Fun House, eh? Haven't really had a chance to talk with you much about that one. That was quite a coup you pulled off there."

I felt warmed and flattered by his comment. While we were technically equals . . . had been for some time . . . he was still my old teacher, and I couldn't help but react to praise from him.

"It seemed like the best route out of a bad situation," I said offhandedly.

"That's right," he nodded. "It's always easier to solve a problem by throwing money at it than by thinking your way out."

Suddenly this no longer sounded particularly complimentary. I felt my pride turning to defensiveness with the speed of a snuffed candle.

"I believe the financial returns to the company have more than justified the wisdom of the investment."

It sounded a little stuffy, even to me. I had noticed that more and more these days I was retreating into stuffiness for defense in situations where I used to whine about my inexperience or lack of working data.

"Well, I've never been one to complain about clearing a profit," Aahz said, flashing one of his ear-to-ear displays of teeth. "Even when it means acquiring a casino we neither want nor need."

This was definitely sounding like a lecture shaping up instead of a testimonial as to what a fine job I had been doing. While I could make time for a chat and would always take time for "atta boys," I was in no mood to have my shortcomings expounded upon.

"What's done is done, and hindsight is academic," I said briskly, cutting short the casino conversation. "What was it you wanted to see me about?"

I almost started fidgeting with the paper on my desk to press the point home that I was busy, but remembered in time that they were the casino financial reports . . . definitely *not* the way to draw conversation away from that particular subject.

"Oh, nothing much," Aahz shrugged. "I was just heading out on a little assignment and thought you might want to tag along."

"An assignment? I haven't given you an assignment."

I regretted the words as soon as I said them. Not only did they sound bureaucratic, they underscored the fact that I hadn't been finding any work for Aahz, despite our heavy work load.

My old mentor never batted an eye at the faux pas.

"It's not really an assignment. More a busman's holiday. I was going to do a little work on my own time. A favor for a friend who can't afford our normal fees."

I should have been suspicious right then. If I'm at all money-grubbing, it rubbed off from Aahz during our association. Anytime Aahz starts talking about giving something away that we could sell, like our time, I should know there's something afoot.

"Gee, Aahz, I don't think I could take the time. I've been really busy."

". . . Levitating pencils and checking for embezzlement of funds that are all gravy anyway?"

His attempt at an innocent smile was short enough of the mark to be a deliberate botch.

"C'mon, Aahz. That's not fair. I *have* been working hard. I just need a break once in a while. That's all."

"My point precisely," my partner said, springing his trap. "It's about time you got out of this office and out in the field before you become a permanent part of that chair. You don't want to get too far out of touch with the troops, you know, and this little chore is just the thing to remind you what it's like to be on assignment."

I could feel myself being outflanked the longer he talked. In desperation, I held up a hand.

"All right, all right. Tell me about it. Who is this friend of yours?"

"Actually, he's more of an acquaintance. You know him too. Remember Quigley?"

"Quigley? Demon hunter turned magician? That Quigley?"

Aahz nodded vigorously.

"That's the one. It seems he's got a problem he's not up to handling himself . . . which isn't surprising, somehow. I thought you might be interested in lending a hand, since we were the ones who set him up for it."

Check and mate.

"Okay, Aahz," I said, looking mournfully at the unfinished work on my desk. "Just let me clear a few things with Bunny, and I'll be right with you."

Aahz's Tale

JAHK HADN'T CHANGED MUCH from our last visit, but then these off-the-beaten-track dimensions seldom do. We were traveling in disguise, which we Pervects have gotten into the habit of doing when visiting a dimension we've been to before, and the Kid picked up the trick from me. You see, contrary to popular belief, Pervects don't like to fight *all* the time, and the second time through a dimension we usually end up in a fight with anyone who recognizes us and figures they're better prepared than the first meeting. This only confirms the belief we hold on Perv that the rest of the dimensions are antisocial and we'd best swing first to get the surprise advantage, not to mention doing our best to discourage off-dimension visitors whenever possible. Our dimension is unpleasant enough without having strange riffraff drifting through stirring up trouble.

Of course, being a Pervect wasn't the only reason certain citizens of Jahk might want to hang our scalps out to dry. The last time we passed through here, we stirred things up pretty well with our surprise entry into their Big Game. As old and cynical as I may be, I have to smile when I think of the havoc we wreaked then.

"How long do you think this problem of Quigley's is going to take, Aahz?" Skeeve said, breaking into my wandering thoughts.

"I really don't know," I shrugged. "I imagine we'll have a better idea once he fills us in on exactly what the problem is."

The Kid stopped in his tracks and scowled at me.

"You mean you agreed to help without knowing what you were volunteering for? Then how did you know we set him up for it?"

Even though Skeeve's proved himself many times over to be a fast learner, there are still times when he can be dense to the point of being exasperating.

"What was Quigley doing when we first met him?"

"He was a demon hunter. Why?"

"And what's he doing now?"

"Last thing we heard, he was holding down a job as Court Magician for Ta-hoe."

"Now what do you suppose prompted him to take up magik for a living instead of sword-swinging?"

"Oh."

He looked a bit crestfallen for a few moments but rallied back gamely.

"I still think you should have found out what the problem was. Once we're in there, there's no telling how long it's going to take, and I can't be away from the office *too* long. I'm really busy these days."

"Well, then," I smiled, "we should probably be hooking up with him ASAP instead of standing here in the street arguing."

The Kid rolled his eyes melodramatically and set off marching down the road again.

Skeeve has changed a lot in the years I've worked with him. When we first met, he was a kid. Now, he's a young man . . . even though I still tend to think of him as "the Kid." Old habits die hard. He's grown from a gangly boy into a youth who has to shave . . . even though it's only necessary occasionally, so he tends to forget until Bunny reminds him. Even more astonishing is how much he's gained in confidence and poise to a point where he's acquired a certain amount of style. All in all, it's been interesting watching my young charge develop over the last few years. I just wish I felt better about the directions he's been developing in.

You see, Skeeve's most endearing trademark has always been that he cared for people . . . really cared. Whether it was his feeling for Garkin when his old teacher died, even though my colleague never really gave the Kid a fair shake as a student, or the lengths he went to to bolster Ajax's sagging ego when the old Archer was doubting his own value in a fight, Skeeve has always had an unerring ability to see the good in people and act accordingly. That's a lot of why I stuck around to work with him . . . as much to learn as to teach.

Lately, however, things seem to be changing. Ever since he has taken the slot as president of our corporation, Skeeve seems to be worrying more and more about business and less and less about people. The others may not have noticed it. Bunny and Tananda have been so busy trying to one-up each other they wouldn't notice if a brass band marched through the room, and Chumley's had his hands full just keeping them apart. Massha and the hoods are big on blind loyalty. They'd probably follow Skeeve right off a cliff without thinking twice or asking question one. Then again, they haven't known him as long or as well as I have and may simply think his current behavior is normal. To me, however, it represents a major change.

This whole casino purchase thing is just one example. The Skeeve I've known would have insisted that Hysterium know all the facts before signing the contract, or at least given him a more generous price for his efforts. Instead, we were treated to a display of opportunism that would make a hardened Deveel haggler envious.

Now, you all know that I have nothing against making a profit, especially a sinfully large one . . . but that's me. Skeeve is supposed to be the counterbalancing humanitarian. While I've been learning about people from him, I'm afraid he's been absorbing the wrong lessons from me . . . or the right one too well.

Anyway, that's why I didn't chuck Quigley's letter in the wastebasket when it got forwarded to us at the Bazaar. I figured it would give me some time alone with Skeeve to find out whether I was just being a Nervous Nelly, or if there was really something to worry about. So far, I was leaning toward the latter.

Fortunately, Quigley hadn't moved. As impatient as the Kid was being, I was afraid he'd back out of the whole deal if we had to take extra time just to run him down. Our knock was answered with a cautious eye appearing at the crack of the door as it opened slightly.

"Oh! I was hoping . . . that is, I was expecting . . . Can I help you gentlemen?"

We had seen the "old man" disguise before, so there was no doubt that it was really Quigley peering out at us.

"It's us, Quigley," the Kid said briskly before I could even say "Hi." "Will you let us in, or should we just go home?"

"Skeeve? Oh, thank goodness. Certainly . . . come right in."

I personally thought Skeeve was being a bit abrupt, and Quigley's fawning over him wasn't going to improve his manners at all.

"Sorry for the reception," the magician said, herding us inside, "but I was afraid it might be one of my creditors."

As he closed the door, Quigley let his disguise spell drop . . . too much effort to maintain, I guess. Viewing his true appearance, I was slightly shocked.

The years had not been kind to our old ally. There were strain marks etched deeply into his face that hadn't been there when we were here before. The place itself seemed the worse for wear. The walls needed painting badly . . . or at least washing, and the furnishings showed signs of being repaired instead of replaced.

"This place is a dump!" Skeeve observed with his newfound lack of diplomacy. "Really, Quigley. If you won't think of yourself, think of the profession. How are people supposed to respect magicians if they see one of them living like this?"

"Ease up, partner," I said softly. "We can't all own casinos. Some of us have had to live in broken-down shacks in the forest . . . or even sleep under trees on the open road."

That earned me a sharp glance, but Quigley intervened.

"No, Skeeve's right. All I can say is that I've tried. That's part of what's gotten me into the mess I'm in. I've overextended my credit trying to keep up a good front, and now it's catching up with me."

"Gee, Quigley, if that's your only problem we can take care of it in no time at all. We can arrange a quick consolidation loan to get the wolves off your back . . . with a slight interest charge, of course. Right, Aahz?"

The possibility of a fast resolution of the problem seemed to brighten Skeeve's mood immensely. I was almost tempted to go along with it, but I had the feeling there was more to the situation than was meeting the eye.

"I dunno, Skeeve. I think I'd like to hear a little more about exactly what the problem is, if it's all right with you."

"C'mon, Aahz. Let's just settle his accounts and split. If we hurry, we can be back at the office by lunch."

While I had tried to be patient, even promised myself to be, his wheedling tones finally got to me.

"Look, *Kid*," I said, using the phrase deliberately. "If you're so all-fired eager to get back, then go! I'm going to give a shot at trying to solve the *real* problem here, if I can ever find out what it is, maybe even without just throwing money at it. Okay?''

It was a cheap shot, but Skeeve had been asking for it. For a minute I thought he was going to take me up on my suggestion and leave, but instead he sank onto a sofa and sulked. Terrific. I turned my back on him and switched my attention to Quigley.

It seemed funny after all these years to take the lead in what was essentially a ''people'' situation. Usually I handled the tactics . . . okay, and occasionally the money . . . and left the people-handling to Skeeve. It was his part of the partnership to keep my abrasive personality from alienating too many people, particularly our friends. With him off in a blue funk, however, the task fell to me, and I was badly out of practice. Heck, I'll be honest, I was never *in* practice for this sort of thing. Ironically, I found myself trying to think of what Skeeve would say and do at a time like this.

''So, Quigley,'' I said, trying to smile warmly, ''what exactly seems to be the problem?'' ·

He fidgeted uncomfortably.

''Well, it's a long story. I . . . I'm not sure where to begin.''

I suddenly remembered that non-Pervects tend to get nervous at the sight of Pervect teeth and dumped the smile.

''Why don't you start at the beginning? How come you're having money problems? You seemed to be doing all right the last time we were here.''

''That's when it started,'' he sighed, ''the last time you were here. Remember how they used to settle who was going to be the government around here? With the Big Game?''

Actually I hadn't thought about it for years, but it was starting to come back to me as he talked.

"Uh-huh. The Big Game between Ta-hoe and Vey-gus each year would decide who would get the Trophy *and* be the capital for the next year."

Quigley nodded vaguely.

"Right. Well, that's all changed now. When you guys won the game and took off with the Trophy, it stood the whole five-hundred-year-old system on its ear. For a while there was a faction that maintained that since you had the Trophy in Possiltum, that's where the capital should be for a year. Fortunately, wiser heads won out."

It was nice to know that there were *some* hassles that passed us by. I noticed that in spite of himself, Skeeve had perked up and was listening as Quigley continued.

"What they finally decided was that a Common Council should run the government. The plan was put into action with equal representation from both city-states, and for the first time in five hundred years the government of the dimension stabilized."

It actually sounded like some good had come out of our madcap caper. That made me feel kind of good. Still . . .

"I don't get it, Quigley. How is that a problem?"

The magician gave a wry smirk.

"Think about it, Aahz. With the feud over between the two city-states, there was no reason to maintain two magicians. It was decided that one would do just fine."

"Whoops," I said.

" 'Whoops' is right. Massha was their first choice. She had served as magician for both city-states at one time or another, and, frankly, they were more impressed with her than with me . . . especially after I let their hostage demon escape at the Big Game. When they went to tell her, though, she had disappeared. That left them with me."

I found myself wondering if Massha had signed on as

Skeeve's apprentice before or after she knew about the organizational change and Quigley getting the boot.

"She's working with us over on Deva," Skeeve commented, finally getting drawn into the conversation.

"Really? Well, I suppose it makes sense. After you've gone as far as you can go on the local level, it's only natural to graduate into the big time."

"I still don't see how you ended up behind the eight ball financially," I said, trying to steer the conversation back on course.

Quigley made a face.

"It's my contract. I ended up having to take a substantial pay cut under the new situation. My salary before was adequate, but nothing to cheer about. Now . . ."

His voice trailed off.

"I don't get it," Skeeve said. "How can you be making less money for serving two city-states than you made working for one?"

"Like I said, it's my contract. There are clauses in there I didn't even know about until the council hit me with them."

"What kind of clauses?" I frowned.

"Well, that the employer has the right to set my pay scale is the biggest one I remember. '. . .According to the need of the community,' and they pointed out that with no feud, my workload, and therefore my pay, should be reduced accordingly. Then there's the 'No Quit' clause . . ."

"The what?"

"The 'No Quit' clause. In short, it says that they can fire me, but I can't quit for the duration of my contract. If I leave, I have to pay my replacement, 'sub-contractor' I think they call it, myself . . . even if they pay him more than they were paying me. That's why I'm stuck here. I can't afford to quit. By the time I got done deducting someone else's wages out of whatever I was earning on my new job, I'd be making even less than I am now. I can't believe I could land a position making more than double what I'm currently earning. Not with my track record.''

For a moment I thought Skeeve was going to offer him a position with our company, but instead he groaned and hid his face in his hands.

''Quig-ley! How could you sign a contract with those kind of terms in it? Heck, how could you sign *any* contract without knowing for sure what was in it?''

''Frankly, I was so happy to find work at all I didn't think to ask many questions.''

''. . . There's also the minor fact,'' I put in, ''that when he was getting started in this game, he was all alone. He didn't have a teacher or a bunch of friends to look over his contracts or warn him off bad deals.''

It was getting harder and harder to keep the Kid from getting too intolerant of other people's mistakes. Even that not-too-subtle admonishment only had partial success.

''Well, he could have asked me,'' he grumbled. ''I could have at least spotted the major gaffes.''

''As I recall,'' I tried again, staring at the ceiling, ''at the time you were working as the Court Magician at Possiltum . . . without any kind of written agreement at all. Would *you* have come to you for contract advice?''

''All right, all right. I hear you, Aahz. So what is it you want me to do, Quigley?''

I caught the use of ''me'' instead of ''us,'' but let it go for the time being.

"Well, it's a little late, but I'd like to take you up on your offer. I was hoping you could look over the contract and see if there's a way out of it. My time is almost up, but I'm afraid they're going to exercise their renewal option and I'll be stuck here for another three years."

"Don't tell me, let me guess," I winced. "It's their option whether or not to renew your contract. You have no say in the matter. Right?"

"Right. How did you know?"

"Lucky guess. I figured it went nicely with the 'No Quit' clause. And I thought slavery had been outlawed . . . ."

"Just exactly what are your duties these days, Quigley?"

Skeeve had been maintaining a thoughtful silence on the sofa until he interrupted me with his question.

"Not much, really," Quigley admitted. "More entertainment than anything else. As a matter of fact, I'm going to have to be leaving soon. I'm due to put on an appearance at the game this afternoon."

"The game?" I said. "They're still playing that?"

"Oh, certainly. It's still the major activity for entertainment and betting around here. They just don't play it for the Trophy, is all. It's been a much less emotional game since you guys trounced the locals, but they still get pretty worked up over it. I'll be putting on the after-game entertainment. Nothing much, just a few . . . ."

I glanced at him when he failed to finish his sentence, only to discover he was snoring quietly in his chair, sound asleep. Puzzled, I shifted my gaze to Skeeve.

"Sleep spell," he said with a wink. "I figured it was only appropriate. After all, I learned that spell on our last trip here after our friend here used it on Tananda."

"Don't you want to hear more about the contract we're supposed to be breaking for him, or at least take a look at it?"

"Don't need to. I've already heard enough to rough out a plan."

". . . And that is . . . ?"

His smile broadened.

"I'll give you a hint."

His features seemed to melt and shift . . . and I was looking at the "old man" disguise Quigley favored for his work.

"We don't want two Quigleys attending the game, do we? The way I see it, the best way to get him out of the contract is to take his place this afternoon."

I didn't like the sound of that.

"You're going to get him fired? Isn't that a bit drastic? I mean, how's it going to look on his resume?"

"Look, Aahz," he snarled. "I was the one who wanted to take the easy out and buy him out of his troubles. Remember? *You're* the one who said there had to be another way. Well, I've got another way. Now are you coming, or do you just want me to tell you how it went after it's over?"

The stadium was impressive no matter how you looked at it. Of course, any time you get nearly 100,000 people together all screaming for blood, it's bound to be impressive. I was just glad that this time they weren't screaming for *our* blood.

There was one bad moment, though. It seems that Quigley/Skeeve as a City-State Official got in free, whereas I, in disguise as an ordinary Joe, had to get a ticket to get past the fences. This was well and good, except that it meant we were separated for a bit. During that time, it suddenly dawned on me that if Skeeve got a little lax or wandered out of range, my disguise spell would disappear, revealing my true identity. As one of the team that trounced the locals and made off with their beloved Trophy, it occurred to me that there could be healthier pastimes than being suddenly exposed in the middle of thousands of hopped-up Game fans. Fortunately, I never had to find out for sure. Skeeve loitered about until I gained admission, and we pushed on together. It did give me pause, however, to realize how much I had grown to depend on the Kid's skills since losing my own powers.

Quigley/Skeeve was apparently well known, and many of the fans called to him as we entered the stadium proper. The salutations, however, were less than complimentary.

"Quigley! How's it going, you old fart?"

"Hey, Quigley! Are you going to do the same trick again?"

"Yeah! Maybe you can get it right this time!"

Each of these catcalls was, of course, accompanied by the proper "Haw, haw, haw!" brays, as can only be managed by fans who have started drinking days before in preparation for *their* role in the game. Maybe Quigley was used to this treatment, but it had been a long time since anyone had spoken to the Great Skeeve like that, and I noticed a dangerous glint developing in his eye that boded ill for whoever he finally decided to focus his demonstration on.

The game itself was actually rather enjoyable. It was a lot more fun to watch when we weren't the ones getting our brains beaten out on the field. I found myself cheering for the occasional outstanding play and hooting the rare intervention of the officials, along with the rest of the crazed mob.

Quigley/Skeeve, on the other hand, maintained an ominous silence. I found this to be increasingly unnerving as the afternoon wore on. I knew him well enough to tell he was planning something. What I didn't know were the specifics of "what" and "when." Finally, as the end of the game loomed close, I could contain myself no longer.

"Say, uh, Skeeve," I said, leaning close so he could hear me over the din of the crowd. "Have you got your plan worked out?"

He nodded without taking his eyes off the field.

"Mind telling me about it?"

"Well, remember how I got fired from Possiltum?" he said, glancing around to see if anyone was eavesdropping.

"Yeah. You told the King off. So?"

". . . So I don't see any reason why the same thing shouldn't work here. I don't imagine that City-State Officials are any less pompous or impressed with themselves than the monarch of a broken-down kingdom was."

That made sense. It was nice to see the Kid hadn't completely lost his feel for people.

"So what are you going to chew them out over? Their treatment of Quigley?"

He shook his head.

"Out of character," he said. "Quigley isn't the type to make a fuss over himself. No, I figured to make the fight the key issue."

"Fight? What fight?"

"The one that's about to break out on the field," Quigley/Skeeve grinned. "The way I see it, these two teams have been rivals for over five hundred years. I can't believe *all* their old grudges have been forgotten just because the government's changed.''

"I dunno, partner. It's been a pretty clean game so far. Besides, it's already a rough contact sport. What's going to start a fight?''

"Most of the contact is around the ball . . . or cube, or whatever they call it. Never did get that straight. This late in the game, all the players are hyped up but not thinking too clearly from butting heads all afternoon. Now watch close.''

He leaned forward to hide his hands, as one finger stretched out and pointed at the field.

There were two particularly burly individuals who had been notably at each other's throats all day, to the delight of the crowd. At the moment, they were jogging slowly side by side along the edge of the main action of the field, watching for the ball/cube to bounce free. Suddenly, one player's arm lashed out in a vicious backhand that smashed into his rival's face, knocking his helmet off and sending him sprawling onto the turf. The move was so totally unexpected and unnecessary that the crowd was stunned into silence and immobility. Even the player who had thrown the punch looked surprised . . . which he undoubtedly was. Nothing like a little tightly focused levitation to make someone's limbs act unpredictably, unless they're expecting it and braced against the interference.

The only one who didn't seem immobilized by the move was the player who had been decked. Like I said, the actual players of the game, unlike their out-of-shape fans, are built like brick walls — with roughly the same sense of humor. The felled player was on his feet with a bounce and launched himself at his supposed attacker. While that party was unsure about the magik that had momentarily seized his arm, he knew what to do about being pummeled, and in no time at all the two rivals were going at it hammer and tongs.

It might have worked, but apparently the teams took whatever truce had been called seriously. Amid the angry shouts from the stands and the referee's whistle, they piled on their respective teammates and pried them apart.

"Too bad, Skeeve," I said. "I thought you had them there."

When there was no response, I glanced at him. Brow furrowed slightly now, he was still working.

The player who had been attacked was free of his teammates. Though obviously still mad, he was under control as he bent to pick up his helmet. At his touch, however, the helmet took off through the air like a cannonball and slammed into the rival team member who had supposedly thrown the first punch. Now helmets in this game are equipped with either horns or points, and this one was no exception. The targeted player went down like a marionette with its strings cut, but not before losing a visible splatter of blood.

That did it.

At the sight of this new attack on their teammate, this time when the ball wasn't even in play, the fallen player's whole team went wild and headed for the now unhelmeted attacker . . . whose teammates in turn rallied to his defense.

Both benches emptied as the reserves came off the sidelines to join the fray . . . or started to. Before they had a chance to build up any speed, both sets of reserves were imprisoned by the glowing blue cages of magikal wards, an application I'll admit I had never thought of. Instead of the fresh teams from the benches, Quigley/ Skeeve took the field.

I hadn't realized he had moved from my side until I saw him vault the low railing that separated the spectators from access to the playing field. The move was a bit spry for the "old man" guise he was using, but no one else seemed to notice.

It was a real pleasure to watch the Kid work . . . especially considering the fact that I taught him most of what he knows. I had to admit he had gotten pretty good over the years.

"STOP IT!! THAT'S ENOUGH!!" he roared. "I SAID, STOP IT!!!"

Still shouting, he waded into the players on the field who were locked in mortal combat. The ones who were standing he crumpled in their tracks with a gesture . . . a gesture which I realized as a simple sleep spell. The others he easily forced apart with judicious use of his levitational abilities. Two players who were grappling with each other he not only separated, but held aloft some twenty feet off the ground. As swiftly as it had started, the fight was stopped, and right handily, too.

As could have been predicted, no sooner had the dust settled than a troop of officious-looking individuals came storming out onto the field, making a beeline for Quigley/ Skeeve. While I may have lost my powers, there's nothing wrong with my hearing, and I was easily able to listen in on the following exchange, unlike the restless fans in the stands around me.

"Quigley, you . . . How dare you interrupt the game this way?"

"Game?" Quigley/Skeeve said coolly, folding his

arms. "That wasn't a game, that was a fight . . . even though I can see how you could easily confuse the two."

"You have no right to . . . Put them down!"

This last was accompanied by a gesture at the suspended players. Skeeve didn't gesture, but the two players suddenly dropped to the turf with bone-jarring thuds that drew the same "Ooooo's" from the crowd as you get from a really good hit during actual play.

". . . As to my rights," Quigley/Skeeve intoned, not looking around, "I'm under contract to use my magikal powers to help keep the peace in Vey-gus and Ta-Hoe. The way I see it, that includes stopping brawls when I happen across them . . . which I've just done. To that end, I'm declaring the game over. The current score stands as final."

With that, the cage/wards began migrating toward their respective tunnels, herding the players within along with them. Needless to say, the crowd did not approve.

"You . . . you can't do that!" the official's spokesman screamed over the rising tide of boos from the stands. "The most exciting plays happen in the last few minutes!"

As a final flourish, Quigley/Skeeve levitated the fallen players on the field down the tunnels after their teammates.

"I've done it," he said. "What's more, I intend to do it at every scheduling of this barbaric game when things get out of hand. My contract is up for renewal soon, and I realized I've been a bit lax in my duties. Consequently, I thought I'd remind you of exactly what it is you're keeping on the payroll. If you don't like it, you can always fire me."

I smiled and shook my head in appreciation. I had to

hand it to the Kid. If attacking the dimension's favorite pastime didn't get Quigley canned, I didn't know what would.

"You shut down the game?"

That was Quigley expressing his appreciation for Skeeve's help.

We were back at his place with our disguises off and the magician revived. Apparently our assistance wasn't quite what he had been expecting.

"It seemed like the surest way to get you out of your contract," Skeeve shrugged. "The locals seem rather attached to the game."

"Attached to . . . I'm dead!" the magician cried with a groan. "I won't just get fired, I'll be lynched!"

The Kid was unmoved.

"Not to worry," he said. "You can always use a disguise spell to get away, or if it'll make you feel better, we'll give you an escort to . . ."

There was a knock on the door.

"Ah. Unless I miss my guess, that should be the Council now. Get the door, Quigley."

The magician hesitated and glanced around the room as if looking for a way to escape. Finally he sighed and trudged toward the door.

"Speaking of disguises, Skeeve . . ." I said.

"Oh, right. Sorry, Aahz."

With an absent-minded wave of his hand we were disguised again, this time in the appearances we used when we first arrived.

"Oh! Lord Magician. May we come in? There are certain matters we must . . . oh! I didn't realize you had guests."

It was indeed the Council. Right on schedule. I snuck a wink at Skeeve, who nodded in encouragement.

"These are . . . friends of mine," Quigley said lamely, as if he didn't quite believe it himself. "What was it you wanted to see me about?"

Several sets of uneasy eyes swept us.

"We . . . um . . . hoped to speak with you in private."

"We'll wait outside, Quigley," Skeeve said, getting to his feet. "Just holler if you need us."

"Well, that's that," I sighed after the door closed behind us. "I wonder what Quigley's going to do for his next job?"

Skeeve leaned casually against the wall.

"I figure that's his problem," he said. "After all, he's the one who asked us to spring him from his contract. I assume he has something else lined up."

". . . And if he doesn't? Quigley's never been big in the planning-ahead department. It won't be easy for him to find work with a termination on his record."

"Like I said, that's his problem," Skeeve shrugged. "He can always . . ."

The door opened, and the Council trooped silently out. Quigley waited until they were clear, then beckoned us inside frantically.

"You'll never guess what happened," he said excitedly.

"You were fired, right?" Skeeve replied. "C'mon, Quigiey, snap out of it. Remember us? We're the ones who set it up."

"No, I wasn't fired. Once they got over being mad, they were impressed by the show of magik I put on at the game. They renewed my contract."

I found myself looking at Skeeve, who was in turn looking back at me. We held that pose for a few moments. Finally Skeeve heaved a sigh.

"Well," he said, "we'll just have to think of something else. Don't worry, Quigley. I haven't seen a contract yet that couldn't be broken."

"Ummm . . . actually, I'd rather you didn't."

That shook me a bit.

"Excuse me, Quigley. For a moment there I thought you said . . ."

"That's right. You see, the Council was impressed enough that they've given me a raise . . . a substantial raise. I don't think I'll be able to do better anywhere else, especially if they ask for a demonstration of my skills. There have been some changes in the contract, though, and I'd really appreciate it if you two could look it over and let me know what I'm in for."

"I'm sorry about that, Skeeve," I said as we trudged along. "All that work for nothing."

We had finally finished going over the contract with Quigley and were looking for a quiet spot to head back to Deva unobserved.

"Not really. We solved Quigley's problem for him, and that new contract is a definite improvement over the old one."

I had meant that he had done a lot of work for no pay, but decided not to push my luck by clarifying my statement.

"You kind of surprised me when we were talking outside," I admitted. "I half expected you to be figuring on recruiting Quigley for our crew, once he got free of his contract."

The Kid gave a harsh bark of laughter.

"Throw money at it again? Don't worry, Aahz. I'm not that crazy. I might have been willing to spot him a loan, but hire him? A no-talent, do-nothing like that? I run a tight ship at M.Y.T.H.´Inc, and there's no room for deadwood . . . even if they are old friends. Speaking of the company, I wonder if there's any word about . . ."

He rambled on, talking about the work he was getting back to. I didn't listen too closely, though. Instead, I kept replaying something he had said in my mind.

"A no-talent do-nothing . . . no room for deadwood, even if they are old friends . . ."

A bit harsh, perhaps, but definitely food for thought.

Chapter Five:

"What fools these mortals be."
—SMAUG

I NEVER REALLY REALIZED how easy it was to buy something until I tried my hand at selling. I'm not talking about small, casual purchases here. I'm talking about something of size . . . like, say, a casino/hotel. Of course buying it had been simplified by the fact that the developer . . . what was his name? No matter . . . was desperate. Trying to offload it, however, was an entirely different matter.

Leaning back in my chair, I stared at the sea of paper on my desk, trying to mentally sort out the various offers, only to discover they were starting to run together in my head. I've noticed that happening more and more after midnight. With a muttered curse, I cast about for my notes.

"Working late, Skeeve?"

"What?" I said, glancing up. "Oh. Hi, Bunny. What are you doing here at this hour?"

"I could say I was worried about you, which I am,

but truthfully I didn't even know you were still here till I saw the light on and poked my head in to check. No, I was just fetching a few things I had stored in my desk. Now, I can return the same question: what are *you* doing here?''

I stretched a bit as I answered, grateful for the break.

"Just trying to organize my thoughts on selling The Fun House. I'm going to have to make my recommendations to the Board as to which of these offers to accept when we discuss it at our monthly meeting.''

She came around the desk and stood behind me, massaging the knots out of my shoulders. It felt wonderful.

"I don't see why you have to make a presentation to the Board at all,'' she said. "Why don't you just go ahead and make the decision unilaterally? You made the decision to sell without clearing it with anyone else.''

Something in what she said had a ominous ring to it, but I was enjoying the backrub too much to pin it down just then.

"I made the decision unilaterally to open our door to offers . . . not to sell. The actual final call as to whether or not to sell, and, which, if any, of the offers to accept, is up to the Board.''

"Then if it's up to them, why are you killing yourself getting ready to make a pitch?''

I knew where she was coming from then. It was the old "you're working too hard" bit. It seemed like I was hearing that from everybody these days, or often enough that I could sing it from memory.

"Because I *really* want this motion to carry,'' I said, pulling away from her. "If there's going to be any opposition, I want to be sure I have my reasons and arguments down pat.''

Bunny wandered back around the desk, hesitated, then plopped down into a chair.

"All right, then rehearse. Tell *me* why you want to sell, if you don't mind giving a preview."

I rose and began to pace, rubbing my lower lip as I organized my thoughts.

"Officially, I think it's necessary for two reasons. First, pretty soon now the novelty of the place is going to wear off, and when it does the crowds . . . and therefore our revenues . . . will decline. That will make it harder to sell than right now, when it's a hot spot. Second, the place is so successful it's going to generate imitators. From what I've been hearing at my 'businessman's lunches,' there are already several plans underway to construct or convert several of the nearby hotels into casinos. Again, it will dilute the market and lower our price if we wait too long."

Bunny listened attentively. When I was done, she nodded her head.

". . . And unofficially?"

"I beg your pardon?"

"You said, 'Officially, etc., etc.' That implies there are reasons you haven't mentioned."

That's when I realized how tired I was getting. A verbal slip like that could be costly in the wrong company. Still, Bunny was my confidential secretary. If I couldn't confide in her, I was in trouble.

"Unofficially, I'm doing it for Aahz."

"Aahz?"

"That's right. Remember him? My old partner? Well, when we were taking care of that little favor for Quigley, he kept needling me about The Fun House. There was a fairly constant stream of digs about 'throwing money

at a problem' and how 'we never planned to run a casino'
. . . stuff like that. I don't know why, but it's clear to
me that the casino is a burr under his saddle, and if it
will make him happy, I've got no problems dumping it.
It just doesn't mean that much to me.''

Bunny arched an eyebrow.

"So you're selling off the casino because you think it
will make your old partner happy?''

"It's the best reason I can think of,'' I shrugged.
"Bunny, he's been a combination father, teacher, coach,
and Dutch uncle to me since Garkin was killed. I've lost
track of the number of times he's saved my skin, usually
by putting his own between me and whatever was incom-
ing. With all I owe him, disposing of something that's
bothering him seems a pretty small payback, but one I'll
deliver without batting an eye.''

"You might try to give him an assignment or two,''
she said, pursing her lips. "Maybe if he were a bit busier,
he wouldn't have the time to brood and fault-find over
the stuff you're doing without him.''

I waited a heartbeat too long before laughing.

"Aahz is above petty jealousy, really,'' I said, wishing
I was more sure of it myself. "Besides, I *am* trying to
find an assignment for him. It's just that Perverts . . .
excuse me, Pervects . . . aren't noted for their diplomacy
in dealing with clients.''

Not wishing to pursue the subject further, I gathered
up a handful of proposals.

"Right now, I've got to go through these proposals a
couple more times until I've got them straight in my
mind.''

"What's the problem? Just pick the best one and go
with it.''

I grimaced bitterly.

"It's not that easy. With some of these proposals, it's like comparing apples and oranges. One offers an ongoing percentage of profits . . . another is quoting a high purchase price, but wants to pay in installments . . . there are a handful that are offering stock in other businesses in addition to cash . . . it's just not that easy to decide which is actually the best offer."

"Maybe I can help," Bunny said, reaching for the stack of proposals. "I've had a fair amount of experience assessing offers."

I put my hand on the stack, intercepting her.

"Thanks for the offer, Bunny, but I'd rather do it myself. If I'm going to be president, I've got to learn to quit relying on others. The only way I'll learn to be self-reliant is to not indulge in depending on my staff."

She slowly withdrew her hand, her eyes searching mine as if she weren't sure she recognized me. I realized she was upset, but, reviewing what I had said, couldn't find anything wrong with my position. Too tired to sort it out just then, I decided to change the subject.

"While you're here, though, could you give me a quick briefing of what's on the dockets for tomorrow? I'd like to clear the decks to work on this stuff if I can."

Whatever was bothering her vanished as she became the efficient secretary again.

"The only thing that's pressing is assigning a team to a watchdog job. The client has a valuable shipment we're supposed to be guarding tomorrow night."

"Guard duty?" I frowned. "Isn't that a little low-class for our operation?"

"*I* thought so," she smiled sweetly, "but apparently you didn't when you committed us to it two weeks ago.

A favor to one of your lunch buddies. Remember?''

''Oh. Right. Well, I think we can cover that one with Gleep. Send him over . . . and have Nunzio go along to keep an eye on him.''

''All right.''

She started to leave, but hesitated in the door.

''What about Aahz?''

I had already started to plunge into the proposals again and had to wrench my attention back to the conversation.

''What about him?''

''Nothing. Forget I asked.''

There was no doubt about it. The staff was definitely starting to get a bit strange. Shaking my head, I addressed the proposals once more.

Gleep's Tale

INEVITABLY, WHEN CONVERSING WITH my colleagues of the dragon set, and the subject of pets was raised, an argument would ensue as to the relative advantages and disadvantages of humans as pets. Traditionally, I have maintained a respectful silence during such sessions, being the youngest member in attendance and therefore obligated to learn from my elders. This should not, however, be taken as an indication that I lack opinions on the subject. I have numerous well-developed theories, which is the main reason I welcomed the chance to test them by acquiring a subject as young and yet as well-traveled as Skeeve was when I first encountered him. As my oration unfolds, you will note . . . but I'm getting ahead of myself. First things first is the order of business for organized and well-mannered organisms. I am the entity you have come to know in these volumes as . . .

"Gleep! C'mere, fella."

That is Nunzio. He is neither organized nor well-mannered. Consequently, as is so often the case when dealing with Skeeve and his rather dubious collection of associates, I chose to ignore him. Still, an interesting point has been raised, so I had probably best address it now before proceeding.

As was so rudely pointed out, I am known to this particular batch of humans, as well as to the readers of these volumes, simply as Gleep. For the sake of convenience, I will continue to identify myself to you by that name, thereby eliminating the frustrating task of attempting to instruct you in the pronunciation of my *real* name. Not only am I unsure you are physically able to reproduce the necessary sounds, but there is the fact that I have limited patience when it comes to dealing with humans. Then, too, it is customary for dragons to adopt aliases for these cross-phylum escapades. It saves embarrassment when the human chroniclers distort the facts when recording the incidents . . . which they invariably do.

If I seem noticeably more coherent than you would expect from my reputed one-word vocabulary, the reason is both simple and logical. First, I am still quite young for a dragon, and the vocal cords are one of the last things to develop in regard to our bodies. While I am quite able to converse and communicate with others of my species, I have another two hundred years before my voice is ready to attempt the particular combination of sounds and pitches necessary to converse extensively with humans in their own tongue.

As to my mental development, one must take into consideration the vast differences in our expected life-span. A human is considered exceptional to survive for a hundred years, whereas dragons can live for thousands of years without being regarded as old by their friends and relations. The implications of this are too numerous to count, but the one which concerns us here is that, while I am perhaps young for a dragon, I am easily the oldest of those who affiliate themselves with Skeeve. Of course, humans tend to lack the breeding and upbringing of my kind, so they are far less inclined to heed the older and wiser heads in their midst, much less learn from them.

"Hey, Gleep! Can you hear me? Over here, boy."

I made a big show of nibbling on my foot as if troubled by an itch. Humans as a whole seem unable to grasp the subtleties of communication which would allow them to ascertain when they are being deliberately ignored, much less what it implies. Consequently, I have devised the technique of visibly demonstrating I am preoccupied when confronted with a particularly rude or ignorant statement or request. This not only serves to silence their yammerings, it slows the steady erosion of my nerves. To date, the technique yields about a twenty percent success ratio, which is significantly better than most tactics I have attempted. Unfortunately, this did not prove to be one of those twenty percenters.

"I'm talkin' ta *you*, Gleep. Now are ya gonna go where I tell ya or not?"

While I am waiting for my physical development to enable me to attempt the language of another species, I have serious doubts that Nunzio or Guido will master their *native* tongue, no matter how much time they are allowed. Somehow it reminds me of a tale one of my aunts used to tell about how she encountred a human in a faraway land and inquired if he were a native. "I ain't no native!" she was told. "I was born right here!" I quite agree with her that the only proper response when confronted by such logic was to eat him.

Nunzio was still carrying on in that squeaky little-boy voice of his which is so surprising when one first hears it, except now he had circled around behind me and was trying to push me in the direction he had indicated earlier. While he is impressively strong for a human, I outweighed him sufficiently that I was confident that there was no chance he could move me until I decided to cooperate. Still, his antics were annoying, and I briefly debated whether it was worth trying to improve his manners by belting him with my tail. I decided against it, of course. Even the strongest humans are dangerously frail and vulnerable, and I did not wish to distress Skeeve by damaging one of his playmates. A trauma like that could set my pet's training program back years.

Right about then I observed that Nunzio's breathing had become labored. Since he had already demonstrated his mental inflexibility, I grew concerned that he might suffer a heart attack before giving up his impossible task. Having just reminded myself of the undesirability of his untimely demise, I decided I would have to humor him.

Delaying just long enough for a leisurely yawn, I rose and ambled in the indicated direction . . . first sliding sideways a bit so that he fell on his face the next time he threw his weight against me. I reasoned that if he wasn't sturdy enough to survive a simple fall, then my pet was better off without his company.

Fortunately or un-, depending on your point of view, he scrambled rapidly to his feet and fell in step beside me as I walked.

"I want youse to familiarize yourself with the shipment which we are to be protectin'," he said, still breathing hard, "then wander around the place a little so's yer familiar with the layout."

This struck me as a particularly silly thing to do. I had sized up the shipment and the layout within moments of our arrival, and I had assumed that Nunzio had done the same. There simply wasn't all that much to analyze.

The warehouse was nothing more than a large room . . . four walls and a ceiling with rafters from which a scattered collection of lights poured down sufficiently inadequate light as to leave large pockets of shadows through the place. There was a small doorway in one wall, and a large sliding door in another, presumably leading to a loading dock. Except for the shipment piled in the center of the room, the place was empty.

The shipment itself consisted of a couple dozen boxes stacked on a wooden skid. From what my nose could ascertain, whatever was inside the boxes consisted of paper and ink. Why paper and ink should be valuable enough to warrant a guard I neither knew nor cared. Dragons do not have much use for paper . . . particularly paper money. Flammable currency is not our idea of a sound investment for a society. Still, someone must have felt the shipment to be of some worth, if not the human who had commissioned our services, then definitely the one dressed head to foot in black who was creeping around in the rafters.

All of this had become apparent to me as soon as we had entered the warehouse, so there was no reason to busy oneself with make-work additional checks. Nunzio, however, seemed bound and determined to prod me into rediscovering what I already knew. Even allowing for the fact that the human senses of sight, hearing, taste, touch, and smell are far below those of dragons, I was nonetheless appalled at how little he was able to detect on his own. Perhaps if he focused less of his attention on me and more on what was going on around us, he would have fared better. As it was, he was hopeless. If Skeeve was hoping that Nunzio would learn something from me, which was the only reason I could imagine for including him on the assignment, my pet was going to be sorely disappointed. Other than the fact that he seemed to try harder than most humans to interact positively with dragons, however crude and ignorant his attempts might be, I couldn't imagine why I was as tolerant of him as I was.

Whoever it was in the rafters was moving closer now. He might have been stealthy for a human, but my ears tracked him as easily as if he were banging two pots together as he came. While I was aware of his presence two steps through the door, I had been uncertain as to his intentions and therefore had been willing to be patient until sure whether he were simply an innocent bystander, or if he indeed entertained thoughts of larceny. His attempts to sneak up on us confirmed to me he was of the latter ilk, however incompetent he might be at it.

Trying to let Nunzio benefit from my abilities, I swiveled my head around and pointed at the intruder with my nose.

"Pay attention, Gleep!" my idiot charge said, jerking my muzzle down toward the boxes again. "This is what we're suppose to be guardin'. Understand?"

I understood that either humans were even slower to learn than the most critical dragons gave them credit for, which I was beginning to believe, or this particular specimen was brain-damaged, which was also a possibility. Rolling my eyes, I checked on the intruder again.

He was nearly above us now, his legs spread wide supporting his weight on two of the rafters. With careful deliberation, he removed something from within his sleeve, raised it to his mouth, and pointed it at us.

Part of the early training of any dragon is a series of lessons designed to impart a detailed knowledge of human weapons. This may sound strange for what is basically a peace-loving folk, but we consider it to be simple survival . . . such as humans instructing their young that bees sting or fire is hot. Regardless of our motivations, let it suffice to say that I was as cognizant of human weapons as any human, and considerably more so than any not in the military or other heroic vocations, and, as such, had no difficulty at all identifying the implement being directed at us as a blowgun.

Now, in addition to having better sense, dragons have armor which provides substantially more protection than humans enjoy from their skin. Consequently, I was relatively certain that whatever was set to emerge from the business end of the blowgun would not pose a threat to my well-being. It occurred to me, however, that the same could not be said for Nunzio, and, as I have said before, I have qualms about going to some lengths to ensure my pet's peace of mind by protecting his associates.

Jerking my head free from Nunzio's grasp, I took quick aim and loosed a burst of #6 flame. Oh, yes. Dragons have various degrees of flame at their disposal, ranging from "toast a marshmallow" to "make a hole in rock." You might keep that in mind the next time you consider arguing with a dragon.

Within seconds of my extinguishing the pyrotechnics, a brief shower of black powder drifted down on us.

"Darn it, Gleep!" Nunzio said, brushing the powder

from his clothes. "Don't do that again, hear me? Next time you might do more than knock some dust loose . . . and look at my clothes! Bad dragon!"

I had been around humans enough not to expect any thanks, but I found it annoying to be scolded for saving his life. With as much dignity as I could muster, which is considerable, I turned and sat with my back to him.

"GLEEP! UP, BOY! GOOD DRAGON! GOOD DRAGON!"

That was more like it. I turned to face him again, only to find him hopping around holding his foot. Not lacking in mental faculties, I was able to deduce that, in making my indignant gesture, I had succeeded in sitting on his lower extremities. It was unintentional, I assure you, as human feet are rather small and my excellent sense of touch does not extend to my posterior, but it did occur to me in hindsight (no pun intended) that it served him right.

"Look, you just sit there and I'll sit over here and we'll get along fine. Okay?"

He limped over to one of the cartons and sat down, alternately rubbing his foot and brushing his clothes off.

The powder was, of course, the remains of the late intruder/assassin. #6 flame has a tendency to have that effect on humans, which is why I used it. While human burial rights have always been a source of curiosity and puzzlement to me, I was fairly certain that they did not include having one's cremated remains brushed onto the floor or removed by a laundry service. Still, considering my difficulty in communicating a simple "look out" to Nunzio, I decided it would be too much effort to convey to him exactly what he was doing.

If my attitude toward killing a human seems a bit

shocking in its casualness, remember that to dragons humans are an inferior species. You do not flinch from killing fleas to ensure the comfort of your dog or cat, regardless of what surviving fleas might think of your callous actions, and I do not hesitate to remove a bothersome human who might cause my pet distress by his actions. At least we dragons generally focus on individuals as opposed to the wholesale slaughter of species humans seem to accept as part of their daily life.

"You know, Gleep," Nunzio said, regarding me carefully, "after a while in your company, even Guido's braggin' sounds good . . . but don't tell him I said that."

"Gleep?"

That last sort of slipped out. As you may have noticed, I am sufficiently selfconscious about my one-word human vocabulary that I try to rely on it as little as possible. The concept of my telling Guido anything, however, startled me into the utterance.

"Now, don't take it so hard," Nunzio scowled, as always interpreting my word wrong. "I didn't mean it. I'm just a little sore, is all."

I assumed he was referring to his foot. The human was feeling chatty, however, and I soon learned otherwise.

"I just don't know what's goin' on lately, Gleep. Know what I mean? On the paperwork things couldn't be goin' better, except lately everybody's been actin' crazy. First the Boss buys a casino we built for somebody else, then overnight he wants to sell it. Bunny and Tananda are goin' at each other for a while, then all of a sudden Bunny's actin' quiet and depressed and Tananda . . . did you know she wanted to borrow money from me the other day? Right after she gets done with that collection job? I don't know what she did with her commission or why she doesn't ask the Boss for an advance or even what she needs the money for. Just 'Can you spot me some cash, Nunzio? No questions asked?', and when I try to offer my services as a confidential type, she sez 'In that case, forget it. I'll ask someone else!' and leaves all huffy-like. I'll tell ya, Gleep, there's sumpin' afoot, and I'm not sure I like it.''

He was raising some fascinating points, points which I'll freely admit had escaped my notice. While I had devoted a certain portion of my intellect to deciphering the intricascies of human conduct, there was much in the subtleties of their intraspecies relationships which eluded me . . . particularly when it came to individuals other than Skeeve. Reflecting on Nunzio's words, I realized that my pet had not been to see me much lately, which was in itself a break in pattern. Usually he would make time to visit, talking to me about the problems he had been facing and the self-doubts he felt. I wondered if his increased absences were an offshoot of the phenomenon Nunzio was describing. It was food for thought, and something I promised myself I would consider carefully at a later point. Right now, there were more immediate matters demanding my attention . . . like the people burrowing in under the floor.

It seemed that, in the final analysis, Nunzio was as inept as most humans when it came to guard duty. They make a big show of alertness and caution when they come on duty, but within a matter of hours they are working harder at dealing with their boredom than in watching whatever it is they're supposed to be guarding. To be honest, the fact that dragons have longer lives may explain part of why we are so much better at staving off boredom. After a few hundred years, days, even weeks shrink to where they have no real time value at all. Even our very young have an attention span that lasts for months . . . sometimes years.

Whatever the reason, Nunzio continued to ramble on about his concerns with the status quo, apparently oblivious to the scratching and digging sounds that were making their way closer to our position. This time it wasn't simply my better hearing, for the noise was easily within the human range, though admittedly soft. By using *my* hearing, I could listen in on the conversations of the diggers.

"How much farther?"

"Sshhh! About ten feet more."

"Don't 'sshhh' me! Nobody can hear us."

"*I* can hear you! This tunnel isn't that big, ya know."

"What are you going to do with your share of the money after we steal the stuff?"

"First we gotta steal it. *Then* I'll worry about what to do with my share."

That was the part I had been waiting to hear. There had always been the chance they were simply sewer diggers or escaping convicts or something equally non-threatening to our situation. As it was, though, they were fair game.

Rising from where I had been sitting, I moved quietly to where they were digging.

". . . unless Don Bruce wants to . . . Hey! Where are you goin'? Get back here!"

I ignored Nunzio's shouting and listened again. On target. I estimated about four feet down. With a mental smirk, I began jumping up and down, landing as heavily as I could.

"What are you doin'? Stop that! Hey, Gleep!"

The noise Nunzio was making was trivial compared to what was being said four feet down. When I mentioned earlier that I was too heavy for Nunzio to move unassisted, I was not meaning to imply that he was weak. The simple poundage of a dragon is a factor to be reckoned with even if it's dead, and if it's alive and thinking, you have real problems. I felt the floor giving way and hopped clear, relishing the sounds of muffled screams below.

"Jeez. Now look what you've done! You broke the floor!"

Again I had expected no thanks and received none. This did not concern me, as at the moment I was more interested in assessing the damage, or lack of damage, I had inflicted on this latest round of potential thieves.

The floor, or a portion of it, now sagged about a foot lower, leading me to conclude that either the tunnel below had not been very high, or that it had only partially collapsed. Either way, there were no more sounds emanating from that direction, which meant the thieves were either dead or had retreated emptyhanded. Having accomplished my objective of removing yet another threat to the shipment, I set my mind once again on more important things. Turning a deaf ear to Nunzio's ravings, I flopped down and pretended to sleep while I indulged in a bit of leisurely analysis.

Perhaps Nunzio was right. It was possible that my pet was reacting adversely to the change in his status from free-lance operator to the head of a corporation, much the same as tropical fish will suffer if the pH of the water in their aquarium is changed too suddenly. I was very much aware that an organism's environment consisted of much more than their physical surroundings . . . social atmosphere, for example, often influenced a human's well-being. If that were the case, then it behooved me to do something about it.

Exactly how I was to make the necessary adjustments would be a problem. Whenever possible, I tried to allow my pet free will. That is, I liked to give him the illusion of choosing his own course and associates without interference from me. Occasionally I would stray from this stance, such as when they brought that horrible Markie creature into our home, but for the most part it was an unshakeable policy. This meant that if I indeed decided that it was time to winnow out or remove any or all of Skeeve's current associates for his own good, it would have to be done in a manner which could not be traced to me. This would not only preserve the illusion that I was not interfering in his life, but also save him the angst which would be generated if he realized I was responsible for the elimination of one or more of his friends. Yes, this would require considerable thought and consideration.

"Here, fella. Want a treat?"

This last was uttered by a sleazy-looking Deveel as he held out a hand with a lump of some unidentifiable substance in it.

I realized with a guilty start that I had overindulged, sinking too far into my thoughts to maintain awareness of my surroundings. After the unkind thoughts I had entertained about Nunzio's attention span, this was an inexcusable lapse on my part. Ignoring the offered gift, I raised my head and cast about desperately to reassess the situation.

There were three of them: the one currently addressing

me, and two others who were talking to Nunzio.

"I dunno," the latter was saying. "I didn't get any instructions about anyone pickin' up the shipment early."

Something was definitely amiss. From his words and manner, even Nunzio was suspicious . . . which meant the plot had to be pretty transparent.

"C'mon boy. Take the treat."

The Deveel facing me was starting to sound a little desperate, but I continued ignoring him and his offering. It was drugged, of course. Just because humans can't smell a wide range of chemicals, they assume that no one else can either. This one was no problem. I was more concerned as to whether or not Nunzio would require assistance.

"I can't help it if your paperwork is fouled up," the smaller Deveel with Nunzio snarled, with a good imitation of impatience. "I've got a schedule to keep. Look. Here's a copy of my authorization."

As Nunzio bent to look at the paper the Deveel was holding, the one standing behind him produced a club and swung it at his head. There was a sharp "CRACK" . . . but it was from the club breaking, not from Nunzio's head, that latter being, as I have noted, exceptionally dense.

"I'm sorry, I can't let you have the shipment," Nunzio said, handing the paper back to the short Deveel who took it without losing the astounded expression from his face. "This authorization is nothin' but a blank piece of paper."

He glanced over his shoulder at the larger Deveel who was standing there staring at his broken club.

"Be with you in a second, fella. Just as soon as we get this authorization thing cleared up."

I decided that he would be able to handle things in his own peculiar way and turned my attention to the Deveel with the drugged treat.

He was looking at the conversation across the room, his mouth hanging open in amazement. I noticed, however, that he had neglected to withdraw his hand.

There are those who hypothesize that dragons do not have a sense of humor. To prove that that is not the case, I offer this as a counterexample.

Unhinging my jaw slightly, I stretched out my neck and took the treat in my mouth. Actually, I took his hand in my mouth . . . all the way to the shoulder. This was not as hazardous as it sounds. I simply took care not to swallow and therefore avoided any dangerous effects which might be generated by the drugged treat.

The Deveel glanced back when he heard my jaws crash together, and we looked into each others' eyes from a considerably closer range than he had anticipated. For effect, I waggled my eyebrows at him. The eyebrows did it, and his eyes rolled up into his head as he slumped to the floor in a dead faint.

Funny, huh? So much for not having a sense of humor.

Relaxing my jaws, I withdrew my head leaving the treat and his arm intact, and checked Nunzio's situation again.

The larger Deveel was stretched out on the floor unconscious while Nunzio was holding the other by the lapels with one hand, leisurely slapping him forehand and backhand as he spoke.

"I oughtta turn youse over to da authorities! A clumsy hijack like this could give our profession a bad name. Know what I mean? Are you listenin' ta me? Now take your buddies and get outta here before I change my mind!

And don't come back until you find some decent help!''

I had to admit that Nunzio had a certain degree of style . . . for a human. If he had been fortunate enough to be born with a brain, he might have been a dragon.

While he was busy throwing the latest batch of attackers out the door, I decided to do a little investigating. After three attempts to relieve us of our prize, though Nunzio was only aware of one of them, I was beginning to grow a bit suspicious. Even for as crime-prone a lot as humans tend to be, three attempts in that close succession was unusual, and I wanted to know more about what it was we were guarding.

The cases still smelled of paper and ink, but that seemed an inadequate reason for the attention they had been drawing. As casually as I could, I swatted one of the cases with my tail, caving it in. Apparently I had not been casual enough, for the sound brought Nunzio sprinting to my side.

''Now what are you doin'? Look! You ruined . . . Hey! Wait a minute!''

He stooped and picked up one of the objects that had spilled from the case and examined it closely. I snaked my head around so I could look over his shoulder.

''Do you know what dis is, Gleep?''

As a matter of fact, I didn't. From what I could see, all it was was some kind of picture book . . . and a shoddily made one at that. What it *didn't* look like was anything valuable. Certainly nothing that would warrant the kind of attention we had been getting.

Nunzio tossed the book back onto the floor and glanced around nervously.

''This is over my head,'' he murmured. ''I can't . . . Gleep, you keep an eye on this stuff. I'll be right back.

I've gotta get the Boss . . . and Guido! Yea. He knows about this stuff.''

Admittedly perplexed, I watched him go, then studied the book again.

Very strange. There was clearly something in this situation that was escaping my scrutiny.

I rubbed my nose a few times in a vain effort to clear it of the smell of ink, then hunkered down to await my pet's arrival.

''Comic books?''

Skeeve was clearly as perplexed as I had been.

''The 'valuable shipment' we're guarding is comic books?''

''That's what I thought, Boss,'' Nunzio said. ''Screwy, huh? What do you think, Guido?''

Guido was busy prying open another case. He scanned the books on top, then dug a few out from the bottom to confirm they were the same. Studying two of them intently, he gave out with a low whistle.

''You know what these are worth, Boss?''

Skeeve shrugged.

''I don't know how many of them are here, but I've seen them on sale around the Bazaar at three or four for a silver, so they can't be worth much.''

''Excuse me for interruptin','' Guido said, ''but I am not referrin' to yer everyday, run-of-the-mill comic. I am lookin' at these, which are a horse from a different stable.''

''They are?'' my pet frowned. ''I mean . . . it is? I mean . . . these all look the same to me. What makes them special?''

''It is not easy to explain, but if you will lend me your

ears I will attempt to further your education, Boss. You too, Nunzio.''

Guido gathered up a handful of the books and sat on one of the cases.

"If you will examine the evidence before you, you will note that while all these comics are the same, which is to say they are copies of the same issue, they each have the number 'one' in a box on their cover. This indicates that it is the first issue of this particular title.''

I refrained from peering at one of the books. If Guido said the indicator was there, it was probably there, and looking at it wouldn't change anything.

"Immediately that 'one' makes the comic more valuable, both to someone who is tryin' to obtain a complete set, and especially to a collector. Now, certain titles is more popular than others, which makes them particularly valuable, but more important are titles which have indeed grown in popularity since they made their first debutante. In that situational, there are more readers of the title currently than there were when it began, and the laws of supply and demand drive the price of a first-issue copy through the roof.''

He gestured dramatically with one of the books.

"This particular title premiered several years ago and is currently hotter than the guy what swiped the crown jewels. What is more, the print run on the first issue was very small, makin' a first-issue copy exceedingly valuable . . . with the accent on 'exceedingly.' I have with my own eyes seen a beat-up copy of the comic you are currently holding on a dealer's table with an askin' price of a hundert-fifty gold on it. Mind you, I'm not sayin' he got it, but that's what he was askin'.''

Now it was Skeeve's turn to whistle. I might have

been tempted myself, but whistling is difficult with a forked tongue.

"If that's true, this shipment is worth a fortune. He's got enough of them here."

"That is indeed the puzzlement, Boss," Guido said, looking at the cases. "If my memory is not seriously in error, there were only two thousand copies of this issue printed . . . yet if all these cases are full of the same merchandise, there are considerably more copies than that in this shipment to which we are referrin'. How this could be I am uncertain, but the explanation which occurs to me is less than favorable to the owner."

"Forgeries!" Nunzio squeaked. "The guy's a multi-colored paper hanger!"

"A multi . . . never mind!" Skeeve waved. "What good would forged comics be?"

"The same as any other forgery," Guido shrugged. "You pass 'em off as originals and split with the money before anyone's the wiser. In some ways it's better'n phony money, since it isn't as hard to duplicate comics and, as youse can see, they're worth more per pound. The paper's cheaper, too."

My pet surveyed the shipment.

"So we've been made unwitting accomplices to a comic-forging deal, eh?"

". . . And without even gettin' a piece of the action," Nunzio snarled.

"That wasn't what I was thinking about," Skeeve said, shaking his head. "I was thinking of all the collectors who are going to plunk down their money to get a genuine collector's item, only to have the bottom drop out of the market when it's discovered that it's been flooded with forgeries."

He rubbed his lower lip thoughtfully.

"I wonder how much my lunch buddy has insured this shipment for?"

"Probably not much, if at all," Guido supplied. "To do so would necessitate the fillin' out of documents declarin' the contents of said shipment, and any insurance type knowledgeable enough to give him full value would also know the discrepancy between the shipment count and what was originally printed. You see, Boss, the trouble with runnin' a fraud is that it requires runnin' additional frauds to cover for it, and eventually someone is bound to catch on."

Skeeve wasn't even listening by the time Guido finished his oration. He was busy rubbing the spot between my ears, a strange smile on his face.

"Well, I guess nobody wins all the time."

"What was that, Boss?"

My pet turned to face them.

"I said that M.Y.T.H. Inc. fumbled the ball this time. Sorry, Nunzio, but this one is going into the records as a botched assignment. I can only assure you that it will *not* be reflected on your next performance review."

"I don't get it," Nunzio frowned. "What went wrong?"

"Why, the fire of course. You know, the fire that destroyed the entire shipment due to our inattentiveness and neglect? Terribly careless of us, wasn't it?"

"Fire? What fire?"

Skeeve stepped to one side and bowed to me, sweeping one hand toward the cases.

"Gleep? I believe this is your specialty?"

I waffled briefly between using a #4 or a #6, then said "to heck with it" and cut loose with a #9. It was a bit show-offy, I'll admit, but with Guido and Nunzio watching, not to mention my pet, it was pointless to spare the firepower.

They were impressed, which was not surprising, as #9 is quite impressive. There wasn't even any afterburn to put out, since by the time I shut down the old flame-thrower, there was nothing left to burn.

For several moments we all stood staring at the charred spot on the warehouse floor.

''Wow!'' Guido breathed at last.

''You can say that double for me,'' Nunzio nodded, slipping an arm around my neck. ''Good dragon, Gleep. Good dragon.''

''Well, gentlemen,'' Skeeve said, rubbing his hands together, ''now that that's over I guess we can head . . . What's that?''

He pointed to the collapsed portion of the floor, noticing it for the first time.

''That?'' Nunzio squeaked innocently. ''Beats me, Boss. It was like that when we got here.''

I didn't bother to return his wink, for I was already starting to retreat into heavy thought. I only hoped that in the final analysis I wouldn't decide that either Guido or Nunzio was an unsettling influence on my pet. Time would tell.

Chapter Six:

"Not everything in life is funny."
—R. L. ASPRIN

THE CREW SEEMED to be in high spirits as they gathered in my office for our monthly board meeting. Congratulations and jibes were exchanged in equal portions, as was the norm, and they began to settle in for what promised to be a marathon session.

I was glad *they* were in a good mood. It might make what I had to say a little easier, though I doubted it. I was still reeling from the one-two punch I had just received, and now it was my job to pass it on to them.

My own view of the pending session was a mixture of dread and impatience. Impatience finally dominated, and I called the meeting to order.

"I know you all came prepared to discuss the sale of The Fun House," I said, looking around at the team members sprawled hither and yon, "but something has come up that I think takes priority over that. If no one objects, I'll temporarily table the casino discussion in favor of new business."

That caused a bit of a stir and an exchange of puzzled glances and shrugs. Not wanting to be sidetracked by a round of questions or comments, I hurried on.

"There's an assignment . . . no, I can't call it that. There's no payment involved and no client. It's just something I think M.Y.T.H. should get involved in. I don't feel I can order anyone to take part . . . in fact, I don't even see putting it to a vote. It's got to be on an individual volunteer basis."

Tananda raised her hand. I nodded at her.

"Do we get to hear what it is? Or are we supposed to volunteer blind?"

I searched for the words for a moment, then gave up. Instead of speaking, I pushed the little oblong box that was on my desk toward her. She frowned at it, glanced at me, then picked it up and raised the lid.

One look inside was all it took for her to get the message. Sinking back in her seat, we locked eyes for a moment; then she shook her head and gave a low whistle.

"I say, is this a private horror, or can any number play?" Chumley grumbled from across the office.

In response, Tananda held up the box, tilting it so everyone could see the contents. Inside was a severed finger, a woman's finger, to be exact. It was wearing a particularly gaudy ring.

There was a long silence as the assemblage stared at the missive. Then Massha cleared her throat.

"How much for just the ring?" she quipped, but from the tone of her voice she wasn't expecting anyone to laugh.

Nobody did.

"I don't get it, Boss," Guido scowled. "Is this supposed to be a joke or sumpin'?''

"You and Nunzio weren't around for the big finale, Guido," I said. "Remember Queen Hemlock? Back on my home dimension of Klah?"

"Sure," he nodded. "She was an okay skirt . . . a little creepy, though."

"I guess it depended on which side of her favor you were on," Tananda commented wryly, tossing the box back onto the table.

I ignored her.

"Bunny, you weren't around for any of this, so . . ."

"I've picked up some of it talking to Chumley," she waved.

"Well, Queen Hemlock had an interesting plan she wanted to put into effect after she married Rodrick: to combine Possiltum's military strength with the wealth of her own kingdom of Impasse and fulfill her lifelong dream of conquering the world. Of course, she also planned to kill Rodrick if he opposed the idea."

I picked up the box and toyed with it idly.

"I thought I had stopped her by giving Rodrick wedding rings that they thought linked their lives, rings that wouldn't come off. The one in the box here is hers . . . of course, she had to cut off her finger to get rid of it. I hadn't anticipated that."

"I rather suspect she wanted her dream more than her finger," Chumley said with a grimace.

"So it would seem," I nodded. "Now she's on the loose, with an army we inadvertently supplied her with back when I was Court Magician of Possiltum. I'm not the greatest military appraiser around, but I don't think there's anything on Klah that can stop her . . . unless M.Y.T.H. Inc. takes a hand in the game."

"What I don't understand," Chumley said, "is why she informed us of the situation via that missive. Wouldn't she be better off unopposed?"

"Don't you know a challenge when you see one, big brother?" Tananda sighed. "Gauntlets are out of style, so she's giving us the finger."

"You all seem ta have a higher opinion of Queenie than I do," Massha spoke up. "Ta me, it looks more like an invitation to a trap. As I recall, old Hemlock wasn't too well disposed toward us when we split. For all we know, her plan may have already run its course . . . in which case we get to be the featured entertainment at the victory celebration."

That hadn't occurred to me. I seemed to be missing a lot lately.

"You may be right, Massha," I said. "Under the best of circumstances, I'm not sure there's anything that can be done. That's why I'm putting it up for discussion. It's my home dimension, and I was the one who contributed to the problem, so my judgment is biased. In many ways, it's a personal problem. I can't expect anyone else to . . ."

"You're talking it to death, Hot Stuff," Massha interrupted. "You're our peerless leader, for better or worse. Just go for it. We'll be right behind you."

I shook my head and held up a restraining hand.

"It's not that simple. First of all, I don't want this to be a group commitment where a dissenting individual has to be an exception or go along with something they don't agree with. That's why I was calling for individual volunteers . . . with no stigma attached to anyone who doesn't want to sign up. Second . . ."

This was the hard part. Taking a deep breath, I plunged into it.

"Second, I won't be along for this one. Something else has come up that takes priority over Queen Hemlock. Now, if she's not that important to me . . ."

"Whoa. Stop the music!" Tananda exclaimed. "I want to hear what this hot deal is you've got going on the side. What's more important to you than defending your own home dimension?"

I avoided her eyes.

"It's not a deal or a job, really. It . . . It's personal. Something I can't delegate. I've got to handle it myself."

"So tell us," she demanded, crossing her arms. "We're family. If nothing else, don't you think we have a right to know what the head man is going to be doing while we're off fighting a war for him?"

I had had a feeling I wouldn't be able to slip this by unnoticed. With a sigh, I dropped the other shoe.

"Look around the room," I said. "Notice anything missing?"

There was a pause as everyone complied. It took a distressingly long time for them to figure it out.

"Aahz!" Chumley said at last. "Aahz isn't here."

"Say, that's right," Massha blinked. "I thought the meeting was a little quiet. Where is old Green and Scaly?"

"Gone."

It took a moment for it to sink in. Then the team stared at each other in shocked silence.

"The note was on my desk this morning," I continued. "It's his letter of resignation from M.Y.T.H. Inc. Apparently he feels that without his powers he's deadwood . . . taking up space without earning his pay. He's packed up and gone, headed back to Perv."

I dropped the paper back on my desk.

"That's why I'm not going after Queen Hemlock myself. I'm going to Perv . . . after Aahz."

The room exploded.

"To Perv?"

"You've got to be kidding, Hot Stuff."

"But, Boss . . ."

"Skeeve, you can't . . ."

"I say, Skeeve. What if he won't come back?"

I homed in on that last comment. As usual, Chumley managed to hit the heart of the matter.

"If he won't come back . . . well, I'll have tried. I've got to at least talk to him. We've been together too long to let it go with a letter. I'm going to Perv to talk with him face to face . . . and I'm going alone."

A new wave of protest rose in the room, but I cut it off.

"When you go after Queen Hemlock . . . excuse me . . . *if* you go after Queen Hemlock, you're going to need all the manpower you can muster. It's bad enough that I can't be there; don't divide your strength more than it already is. Besides . . ."

My voice faltered a little here.

"This is my problem . . . I mean *really* my problem. I've been doing a lot of thinking since I read this note, and the problem is bigger than Aahz."

I swept the assemblage slowly with my eyes.

"I've gotten pretty wrapped up with being president lately. It's been hard to . . . I've been trying to justify the faith you all have in me by making the business go. In the process, it's gotten so I'm pretty sparse with my 'thank yous' and 'atta boys,' and I've all but lost contact with all of you outside of a business context. Aahz has been my best friend for years, and if he . . . Let's just say I'll be looking for myself as much as for Aahz."

There was dead silence as my oration ground to a halt.

If I had been hoping for any protests over my analysis,
I was playing to the wrong audience. Suddenly, I wanted
the meeting to be over with.

I cleared my throat.

"I'm taking a leave of absence to find Aahz. No discussion is required or allowed. Now, the subject at hand
is whether or not M.Y.T.H. Inc. is going to attempt to
stop Queen Hemlock's assumed attempt to take over
Klah. Are there any volunteers?"